Behind
the
Masque

Philip Wickham

All moral rights of the author have been asserted.
Set in 10.5pt Palatino Linotype & Century Gothic.
Typeset by Mad Goat Media.
A CIP catalogue record for this title is available from the
British Library.

Title:
Behind the masque

Author:
Philip Wickham

Jacket image
by
Philip Wickham

Acknowledgements

My grateful thanks go out to:

Althea Carrington
Owner of the
Courtyard Coffee House
&
Manager, Holly

Dr Sophie Thérèse Ambler
For her empirical research in Medieval History

Fiona Sullivan

By the same author:

The Summerhouse

Undisclosed Advocate

To Walk in Blue Light

Walking Upside Down

In the Screaming Silence

On the Other Side of No Tomorrow

Lime Twigs and Dancing Iguanas

Beyond the Green Shuttered Room

The Avital Shroud

The Squaring of the Circle

Marshmallow Moon *et*
Fleurs de Lumière

In the Silence of Trees

The Settling of the Dust

The Beekeeper

Poetry
Collected Poems
Travel
To Treno Peloponnesus: *A Greek Journey*

For
Jo Hilditch

Behind the masque

behind the masque

Words can be kindly, reassuring and comforting: words that can wrap around you like a warm duvet. Words can also be cruel, sadistic and harming: words that can cause anxieties and distress; for the longest time.

Words sometimes, when strung together in a certain way, can be life changing. They can alter your direction and the path you walk in life.

The latter, was how my life took on a dramatic and unexpected transformation, and where my journey began...

CHAPTER ONE

Monday 23rd May 2022 Paris, France

The taxi journey from Charles de Gaulle was chaotic, rather dull and took longer than my flight from Manchester Airport to Paris. In France, the Covid pandemic restrictions had been lifted on the 11th May 2022, which had allowed me to undertake the journey. My name is Alice Garner and I'm twenty-five years old. I had left my family home in Knutsford, Cheshire, where I live with my parents, Andrew and Eve and my sister Chloe. She is twenty-four and a fourth year medical student at Manchester University.

I'm a writer, well I use the term writer which means rather generally, someone who has written something, which could be almost everybody on the planet. I'm not a columnist or write articles for journals or magazines, or critical pieces or analysis,

I am a novelist, and that's what I write. That brings me to the reason for my visit to Paris. I had received an email from Shakespeare and Company Bookstore Paris, inviting me to place one of my novels into their own reading library. Shakespeare and Company, is without doubt one of the most iconic bookstores worldwide. It was an absolute thrill, honour and privilege to have been asked, and the thought of one of my scribbling's sitting on their personal library shelves, was, and is, such a high. I am not a well-known or renowned novelist; I, like most authors, just sit and scribble into the early hours, or sit for long periods waiting for the next clever thought to come along. In fact, I once wrote somewhere, "One thing to which I am grateful, is that my work slumbers on sweetly, not yet discovered, and shall not conjure that spectre, of being forgotten." You see, for me at least, it is not about sales, money or fame; it is about storytelling. I love the idea that people can be absorbed and captivated by my words and narrative; that they step inside my books and are lost. That thought, inspires and motivates me to continue to breathe life into those characters that have yet to live.

As we drove by the prominent architectural façade of Gare du Nord, we were well and truly in the arrondissements of Paris and the backdrop became much more interesting...until the traffic came to a total standstill.

I eventually arrived at my hotel, which is located about two minutes walk from Notre Dame Cathedral and the River Seine; the same distance, give or take, to Shakespeare and Company.

I had been to Paris once before, in fact it was whilst sitting in the reading library of Shakespeare and Company on my first visit there, that had inspired the book. Serendipity I guess you could say, as I felt it was going home. I remember walking through the bohemian, narrow labyrinthine passageways and turning left and right through an enchanted warren of books telling their own chronicles, storylines, tales, poetry, art, fiction and non-fiction, before walking up a flight of stairs to the reading library. In there, the strangest and unexpected thing happened. Looking at the books stacked all around me, the words seem to drop from the pages and the noise became intense. I sat down in an old leather chair; then a calmness descended, and the words began to tell their own stories and narrative. I had walked inside, and was lost in that magical space...and was happy to be so.

11

I paid the driver and checked into my hotel. It was to be a flying visit – two nights, as I had to be back home for a dental appointment.

The time was 16:48. I had a quick freshen up, a change of top and left my clothes in the open suitcase on the hotel's folding luggage rack to be unpacked later, as I didn't want to waste any time in dropping off the book.

I walked by the Seine briefly, before dropping down a slight incline onto the cobble sets of *Rue de la Bûcherie*. I entered the bookstore and noticed that the guy on the till was in deep concentration searching through their database for a book for a female customer who was looking pensive yet hopeful. Looking around the bookstore, I noticed a girl stacking a few books onto one of the shelves. She was rather tall, which I guess is an asset in a bookstore with so many high shelves, niches, nooks and crannies.

'Hi.'

She turned.

'Oh hello. Can I help you?' she asked easily and with a pleasantly warm smile. I detected a slight American accent.

'American?'

She smiled.

'I'm Canadian,' she said with an impish smile.

12

'Sorry,' I said, with a slight embarrassment.

'That's perfectly fine,' she said pleasantly. 'It happens quite a lot. How can I help you?'

'My name is Alice Garner. I've received a few emails from your News department about one of my novels for your reading library.'

Her face became illuminated.

'*Wow*. How *wonderful*.'

I was a little taken aback by her reaction to be honest.

'You have written it?' she asked with a beam of a smile.

'Well…yes,' I replied, rather indifferently. I guess it was the Parisian traffic that had dulled my senses a little.

'That's fabulous.'

I held up a small gift bag that had written on the front, "for you". I passed it to her.

'Inside the book, I've put in a copy of the emails from you, just to explain why the book is here in the bookstore. I know how big this place is, and I thought…well, you know.'

'That's a *good* idea. I wouldn't want it to be misplaced. To be honest, I'm not sure what to do with it. If you can wait for a few moments, I'll ask my manager.'

I nodded and smiled.

'Yes. Of course.'

She disappeared enthusiastically around one of the corners and down a passageway.

As promised, a few moments later…

'That's fine,' she said with a beam of a smile. The reading library is undergoing some renovation work at the moment, so my manager has put your book with the others that will be returned to the library as soon as the building work is completed.' Once again she gave me a broad and reassuring smile. 'It'll be nice and safe.'

I returned a good-natured smile.

'Thank you so much for your help.'

'It's my pleasure.'

I was just about to turn to leave when…

'It's quite a thing you know.'

I was a little puzzled, and then understood her sentiment.

I nodded and smiled.

'I know. It's a real high point for me. If I never sell another book; it doesn't matter. To have one of my books sitting here is just such a thrill. I can't see it getting any better than that for an author.'

She smiled cheerfully.

'I'm sure that Sylvia (Sylvia Whitman the bookstore owner) would be equally thrilled to hear that. I'll pass that on to her if that's OK?'

I nodded heartily.

'Yes yes. Of course. Please do.'

She nodded cheerily.

'Well, goodbye then,' I said.

'Yes. Goodbye. It was lovely to meet you.'

'You too,' I said with a heartfelt smile.

I exited the bookstore and as I was feeling rather peckish I thought I'd get something to eat at the Shakespeare and Company's café. I walked in and in front of me there were only a couple of people waiting to be served. I imagined that in the height of summer, people would be queuing out the door and beyond. As I waited, I looked around for a vacant table. There was one in a corner by a window, but looking to the outside seating, I fancied alfresco.

'Hello,' said a smiley, chirpy English girl who was probably about my age.

'Hello,' I replied, with a smile.

'What can I get you?'

The small queue whilst waiting to be served, had allowed me just enough time to take a look at the menu board.

'I'd like the quiche, sautéed potatoes and side salad please.'

'Sure. Would you like a drink?'

'Café au lait please.'

'Would you like anything else?' she asked, politely.

'No thank you.'

'Are you sitting inside?'

I pointed to a table outside.

'Just there would be fine.'

She leaned over to read the table's number, and then added it to my order.

'And your name please.'

'Alice.'

'Would you like your coffee now or with your food?'

'Erm, I'll have the coffee now please. That would be great.'

'Sure. That would be eighteen euros please.'

I reached into my bag, took out twenty euros and handed it to her.

'Thank you,' I said.

Thank you,' she replied as she handed me my change.

She passed the order to a young guy; I'd say he was a couple of years younger than the girl. Smiling, she turned back to me.

'We'll bring the food out to you when it's ready. It shouldn't be too long a wait.'

'OK. Thank you.'

I moved to the end of the counter to wait for my coffee as the next customer stepped up to place her order, whilst keeping a fleeting eye out that my chosen table wasn't poached.

I collected my coffee and sat down at my table. It was just lovely; the Gothic quarter, cobbled street, low hedgerow and trees, the quaintness of the bookstore and café and a view of Cathédrale Notre Dame – although covered in scaffolding after the great fire, it was just so relaxing…and so French. I was surprised just how private the café was considering that the main boulevard *Quai de Montebello*, ran on the other side of the hedging.

About ten minutes had passed when…
'Alice?'
I turned; a waitress was stood at my table holding a tray that had my food on board.
I smiled.
'Yes. Thank you.'
She beamed a smile as she placed the food and drink on to my table.
'Enjoy,' she said, with a hint of an eastern European accent.
'Thank you so much.'
Once again the lovely smile.
'You're welcome.'
Although I had only been in Paris for a few hours; as I unfurled the cutlery from the napkin, I thought about the fusion of nationalities that seemingly intermingle so easily in Paris. Whilst waiting for my food to arrive, I had heard *so* many different

17

languages as people walked by and took a selfie or seized a group photo opportunity whilst admiring the iconic bookstore; creating and sharing a happy memory or two; which included taking a couple myself. For some strange reason, my mind reached back to another, and altogether different time: a time of war, fear, mistrust and little acceptance of other nationalities or ethnicities. Society and tolerances of other cultures and traditions in the Paris of the late nineteen-thirties and early nineteen-forties, would have felt like a very different place indeed. Hard to get your head around when you are sipping a café au lait and eating quiche by the same banks of the River Seine in a seductive, ambient sense of mindfulness; which makes you feel safe and so at ease with yourself and the world.
I finished off the food and coffee and sat for fifteen minutes or so just soaking up the atmosphere.

I slipped a five euro note under my plate, stood, pushed my chair back under the table and headed off to my hotel to shower and freshen up before going out for the evening.

CHAPTER TWO

It was a quarter past nine when I left the hotel and went for a walk in and through the narrow streets and alleyways of the Latin Quarter or more precisely, *Quartier Latin*, browsing the many artisan craft shops, usual tourist gift shops, clothes shops and many café bars and restaurants offering French and diverse international cuisines. I loved the feel of the place; a real sense of history, robust yet sympathetically designed architecture; a noticeable pride of being French and I would say patriotism over nationalism, showing acceptance of, and welcoming, its visitors.

Looking more specifically for somewhere to sit and drink a glass or two of vin rouge, I came to Café Paris de V. A piano bar. The music that was drifting out through the doors seemed to hit the right spot for me. I sat down at a table quite near to the grand piano and male pianist. He was good looking, had a shock of brown hair and looked to be in his mid-twenties, and was as cool as the jazz music he was playing. A girl came over to my table and spoke in English with a noticeable French accent. For some reason, she surprised me. I don't know why, but I always presume that the staff that works in the bars and restaurants in Paris would expect you to try to understand and speak a little French.

'Bonjour. Would you like a menu?' she asked, with a wonderful warm smile that lit up her face.

I wasn't really hungry, but I found her easy smile enchanting.

'Er Oui. Yes, please.'

She smiled again and handed me a menu.

'I'll give you a few moments to decide.' She turned and went back to the bar.

I selected a combination of a freshly baked baguette and various cheeses.

The waitress had picked up on my expression and came across once again to my table.

'You are ready to order?'

'Yes please.'

She took out a note pad and a pencil from behind her right ear. It was such a refreshing change from the ubiquitous iPad: the ambiance of the bar, the

21

piano music and the old-fashioned pencil and pad was just right. It set the mood for the night.

I gave her my food order and added my first glass of Vin rouge...I say first, as I had no expectation of leaving Café de Paris V, any time soon.

The music seemed to get better and better and in-between the short breaks, I listened into the various conversations coming from the other patrons. I have always loved travelling on my own. It offers you time to take in the whole view, the conversations and gather your own thoughts without being distracted by small talk...or maybe that's a little unfair, but when travelling with friends or family, you do tend to miss the finer detail of things. You see a partial view or hear a snippet of conversations that surround you, before you have to leave it to answer a question, share an opinion, retell a story or relive a memory. Don't get me wrong; I'm not a loner; I absolutely enjoy the company of others, but equally, there are times when I delight in my own space.

Before I knew it, it had just turned Eleven pm. The pianist was now accompanied by a French female singer...equally as cool and good looking as the pianist. She was French, and sang in French, which I was so glad she did. Now, I really did feel as though I was in Paris. She sang in that very jaunty, and occasional, emotional sensuality that's so evocative of French female singers. A few artistes, of which there are so many, that come to mind are: Vanessa Paradis, Zaz, Tatiana Eva-Marie, Élisabeth Anaïs, and the wonderful and sadly much-lamented, Belle du Berry. Although I can understand, read and speak a little French, I didn't really get the lyrics or the story she was telling; but I'm glad I couldn't, as the words may have distracted me from the feel and ambiance of the soundscape that they created.

After my third glass of wine, I decided, that as it had been such a long and eventful day, I would head back to my hotel. I always feel a gratification when I can infill most of a day with meaningful undertakings and hopefully surprising and new experiences.

The following day however, was to be *too* surprising: an unforeseen occurrence that was to shake my very existence, and whose consequence was to change the path, and course of my life…

23

CHAPTER THREE

After showering and a good hotel breakfast, I decided to put my one full day left in Paris, to good use.

I tend to like to find my own way around places; sometimes it works out well, and others, not so well. I thought as Paris is a warren of narrow streets, alleyways and wide boulevards, that I'd keep the river in view and use it as a guide. I crossed the *Quai de Montebello*, took a couple of photos of Notre-Dame; walked down the steps at the side of the Petit Pont and set off walking along the banks of the river Seine in the general direction of the *Museum national d'Histoire naturelle*. I can say that with confidence, as there was a signpost saying so. As I walked along the Seine, cinematic images came to mind: images from many films, not only French films, but international films. The Seine has been used many times as the backdrop, or even as the main character, in so many films that I have watched. I had a strange feeling of familiarity; as if being reacquainted with a place that I knew so well; as if meeting up with an old acquaintance.

My walk continued as I approached the tourist, river cruise boat, the Batobus. A crewmember had just secured the bowline to a capstan and was opening the gate to allow the passengers to embark or disembark depending on where they had decided to visit. It's a hop-on hop-off cruise; with one ticket, you choose when and where you go along the course of the river. Fabulous idea. One I promised myself, I would use next time I came to Paris for sure. I took a couple of pictures to remind me to do so. I walked on a little further before sitting on a bench where the Seine widens and divides from two-way to a one-way system. The houses across the river were magnificent. Architecture that is a statement of classic grandeur, pride, well-thought out design and built to last…timeless you might say. As I sat there, an idea for a new novel began to form. I had no intention of seeking out any ideas for a new book, however, it's understandable I guess, how the atmosphere and character of the place, can be inspiring to artists, musicians and writers. It's little wonder really that Paris became attracted to, and became a home to many bohemians; as it still does.

After sitting a little while longer contemplating, formulating a new plot and peeling off a couple of photographs; I stood and continued on my way.

I followed the steps leading up from the river to the *Pont d'Austerlitz*. I looked around me and noticed a signpost: *Jardin des Plantes*. I know Jardin means garden, so I fancied taking a look at that. I crossed the busy *Quai Saint-Bernard* and went on into the gardens. It was free on entry, as so many gardens are in and around Paris. It looked so beautiful; well maintained and cared for; once again, that French sense of pride was so obvious.

Wandering around the many flower borders and tree lined paths, I came to a bench, opposite was a structure that looked like a small round and conical roofed, summerhouse. It seemed to me to be just the right spot to sit for a while.

I watched as children played, people having conversations on their mobiles, some so completely consumed by the narrative; gesturing, shrugging and becoming animated, that they were entirely missing the setting of beauty, serenity and scenery that is nature's backdrop. Maybe over time, they have become blasé; it's easy to become so with the familiar I guess. In other quieter places, lovers sat under trees or on the grass making promises to each other that I hope becomes future realities for them…although I have to say that my experiences, so far at least, has proved to be the antithesis. Still, I wished them *Bonne chance*. A man with a calm, softly spoken French voice, spoke to me. I turned to see a middle-aged man dressed in a younger fashionable way, that he was quite able to carry off.

'Excuse me. May I sit here?'

It was a large enough bench, so…

'Yes of course.'

He smiled warmly.

'Merci.'

He politely sat at the other end of the bench, so as not to invade my space.

We both sat there for a few minutes, then he spoke again.

'It's beautiful here isn't it.'

'Yes. Yes it is. So peaceful.'

He smiled sincerely.

We sat unspoken for a further few minutes. I was contemplating to take myself off and find a restaurant for lunch. At that point, the man stood. I looked at him and smiled and I was just about to say "Au revoir", when he spoke once again; in the same softness of voice, but this time his expression took on one of deep sincerity and meaningfulness.

'You are not who you think yourself to be Alice.'

I could neither reply nor react. I was utterly and quietly stunned.

He turned, and slowly walked away.

I was still so taken aback by what he said and how he said it, that I couldn't even shout after him.

I sat there momentarily frozen to the bench; then the reality came over me. I knew I had to find out what he meant, and who he was. I looked for him but couldn't see him anywhere. He had vanished. I stood and followed in his direction, all the time cursing myself for not being more decisive and quicker to react. But how *does* one react to such an extraordinary happening; something *so* unexpected, that it shuts down all of your reactions and thought processes…you become physically and emotionally numb. Who *was* this man that had just entered my life in such a way? How *dare* he say those words and walk away without explanation. I had to sit down once again on a bench to gather my thoughts. I felt angry that this man had walked into my life and changed my perspective…my innocent and uncluttered reverie. I'm a novelist; I *write* this stuff! This however, was not fiction. So I began to look at it as far as I could, through the eyes of a novelist; imaginatively, inventively, yet analytically.

My first thought was that he is some kind of weirdo who had possibly overheard my name at the hotel reception or at Shakespeare and Company when I gave my name when ordering my food; or maybe he was sitting outside when the waitress said my name at the table? That to me at least was plausible. There are such strange people around. I didn't really like that deduction, as the thought that he might be stalking me made me feel very uneasy indeed. But what if, however, there was a darker truth in what he said, and who that shadowy figure is and what he represents. What if it really was some kind of knowledgeable enlightenment? I didn't much like that scenario either; if fact, I liked it less so. I thought about his words…

"You are not who you think yourself to be Alice."

What does that mean; and how do I even begin to interpret that? Taking the first scenario; let's just imagine that he stumbled across my name and just took it upon himself, either through some mental health issue or syndrome, to latch on to me; or more chillingly, callously getting off on wanting to instil fear and anxiety. If that were the case, at least I would be going home the next day.

So, lunatic or prophet? When he spoke those words, he looked so plausible; but then again, I have created a couple of characters in my books that are plausible and turn out to be total psychopaths. My mind was in a spin. Occasionally, the misfortune of being a novelist; is that I have *too* much imagination. Bizarrely, the more I thought about the situation, the hungrier I became. I stood up and set off walking to find a nice café or restaurant.

I didn't retrace my steps along the river bank as I wanted to take a look at the local artisan market stalls that were set up against the river embankment walls by the *Quai Saint-Bernard* and *Quai de Montebello.*

Whilst browsing I remembered seeing a corner café near to Shakespeare and Company. I liked the idea of corner cafés, as I'm a little nosey and if you can get the right table, they offer different viewpoints. I crossed the road and dropped on to cobbled *Rue de la Bûcherie*. I gave a small contented smile as I walked by the bookstore. Just a few steps on, I came to the café Le Petit Pont. An aproned waiter stood smartly by the outside tables offering an easy welcoming smile in order to entice customers into the café. The well-practiced smile of course, gives the impression of cosiness, relaxation and the promise of attentive and respectable service.

From my expression, and that I was looking at the menu, it was fairly obvious to him that his smile had won me over.

'Bonjour,' he said, smartly and kindly. 'You would like a table?'

I nodded.

'Bonjour. Yes, please.' I pointed to an inside corner table by the window. 'Is that table free?'

'Yes of course. Follow me please.'

I followed dutifully; my stomach sending small trills to my brain in the knowledge that it would soon be filled and satisfied.

He pulled out a chair for me. Once again his reassuring smile giving me confidence in the meal to come.

'We have the menu, and also specials of the day,' he pointed to the wall behind the bar, 'just there.'

I nodded and smiled.

'Thank you.'

I ordered a fish dish from the specials board and added a glass of white wine.

The waiter's smile and assumptions of good food and service had not disappointed. It was delightful as was the service. Added to that, I was not hurried to leave. The calm atmosphere and smooth jazz music playing in the background, gave the café a lovely feel. My stomach now happy and content, I sat sipping the rest of my wine; my thoughts returning to the man in the gardens. I decided that he was just a random loony and drew a line under it. It did however, give me an idea for a new novel, replacing the one I'd had earlier sat by the river. I nodded my head self-assuredly.

'Yeah. Why not.' I murmured to myself.

I signalled the waiter for the bill. He nodded, and within a few moments he was at the table and placed the bill on the tabletop. I already knew how much the total was...I'm a bit on it like that. I offered the card to the card reader. He gave me the receipt. I reached into my pocket, pulled out a five euro note and gave it to him. He looked genuinely pleased.

'Merci beaucoup. Thank you very much. You are most kind.'

'You're welcome. The food was delicious. Could I ask you to take a photograph of me?'

He gave a big beam of a smile.

'Of course.'

I set up my phone and passed it to him.

'If you could get some of the café in as well, that would be great.'

I gave the usual cheesy grin and he took the photo. He passed it to me.

'Is it OK?'

I looked at it.

'Perfect. Thank you.'

'My pleasure.'

As I stood, he politely moved the chair out for me.

'Au revoir, and thank you.'

'Au revoir,' I replied. I left the café happy that I had eaten some lovely food and come up with a storyline for a new novel. Inadvertently, the man in the gardens had set me off nicely on a new book.

If only I knew then, what I know now, I would not have been so complacent and I might add, slightly smug, about the encounter and the subsequent altered résumé he gave concerning the truth about who I am, that I, rather foolishly, did not heed…

CHAPTER FOUR

Tuesday 24th May 2022
15:20, Paris

I'm not big on the greasepaint thing, and try wherever I can, to use ethical products. So, after a quick touch-up of lippy and a general freshen up. I looked at my phone: it was 15:20. I left the hotel.

As I had little time left in Paris, I had to make a choice of where to see before my fight home.

I decided to get a taxi to see Eiffel's Tower. Two reasons really, the first, is that I have always wanted to see it, especially lit up at night, and secondly, my novel that had now taken up residency on the shelves of the reading library in Shakespeare and Company - the title of which is: Marshmallow Moon *et* Fleurs *de* Lumière Parts I & II, whose characters exists in a parallel multiverse, where the Paris of the book is similar to the Paris that exists here in our universe; but one where there are subtle, and not so subtle, and surreal differences.

I think it's OK here at this point, to take a small detour and insert into my story a short chapter from Marshmallow Moon, as this piece is the second reason for my wanting to visiting the Tower. It's out of context of course, but I hope you'll see why and stay with it…

The day of the sausage shaped buoyancy aid ensemble

Outside on the street, with the word Fire beam still sounding in his ears and, if it were true, her telling revelation about Aimée; Henri stepped up to the iris recognition scan; the vector, particle, energy-field made a "beep" sound, he stepped on to the Pedeconveyor (*Pedeconveyor is a form of horizontal street escalator that runs alongside main arterial roads and pavements*) and pressed the number of his destination stop. He was on his way to meet Luiz and Celeste at the top of the Eiffel tower as Luiz had something of a revelatory nature to discuss and always found it easier to talk about such things at a greater and higher altitude than sea level. Henri thought that it had come from a sense of excitement and exhilaration when travelling at height whilst riding the wall of death.

Henri felt that he had to be careful with his feelings now, as a lot had changed for him: his love for Celeste – although he would always love her, but no longer in the way that he would have wished it to be. He had always thought that he wanted her to see him young and see him old; that he had loved her for a lifetime...and loved her still. But his passionate love would now live on in the shadowlands, replaced by the closeness, intimacy and warmth of friendship; not a too displeasurable substitute he thought to himself as he smiled contentedly. But now, *Aimée*? This had come completely out of the azure; added to that, he unexpectedly found himself being attracted to Élise. He didn't know why exactly? Whether the attraction was physical; her interesting hair with its captivating "option one option two" thing...maybe; or that she could converse with his gramophone and levitate.

He soon arrived at his stop. He stepped off and made his way to the Eiffel Tower. He took the glass elevator, and as it began to move and ascend the

180 meters of the dramatic, iron lattice construction, he removed a small bag of marshmallows from his pocket. He loved the way his tummy moved around when eating marshmallows when travelling upwards in that particularly long accent. He found it a most pleasing sensation. However, the combination of upwards movement, marshmallow and the motion that his internal organs made to allow him the engrossing feeling of butterflies fluttering in his stomach, did give him the most uncontrollable urge to fart. "For every action there is a reaction" he thought to himself as his expression contorted into some very interesting facial gymnastics as he tried desperately to hold in the gas until he was top side...for all his efforts, it did not end well!

Once at the top, the elevator door and gate opened, allowing a swoosh of fresh air into the lift, for which the others were grateful; he stepped out onto the platform. There were very few tourists there, and as it was to turn out, it was probably just as well.

He found Luiz and Celeste around the other side from the elevator. It was a quiet spot as most people wanted to see the view over the Arc de Triomphe, Notre Dame or the Avenue de Champs Elysees.

'Hello Henri,' said Luiz excitedly.

38

Celeste smiled. She walked over to him.

'Hello Henri,' she said in a warm voice that even though the situation had changed for him, his skin rippled with little electrical quivers, that were wonderful and very therapeutic. He juddered noticeably, which Celeste put down to it being a little chilly.

'Hello Celeste. How are you?'

She smiled and nodded.

'I'm very good Henri. And you?'

He nodded and smiled.

'Yes. The same Celeste.'

Henri couldn't help but notice the rather strange trousers that Luiz was wearing. They reminded him a little of the pants that the Gaucho of the Pampas wear. Giving his legs the appearance of two large sausages. His shirt also looked as though it was straining from some undergarment.

He looked at him with a slight puzzlement; his head tipped slightly to one side.

'You are wondering about my clothing are you not Henri?'

'As am I,' said Celeste.

Luiz gave them both a hauntingly strange smile.

'This may come as some surprise to you Henri. But there is another amongst us that has the skill to conceive ideas and creative invention and creation.'

Henri and Celeste looked at his clothing.

39

'Hmm,' sighed Celeste. 'I'm not sure that this will make you your fortune Luiz.'

He smiled again.

'With all respect. You don't know what it is that I've created yet Celeste.'

Henri narrowed his eyes inquisitively.

'Tricky thing...inventing Luiz.'

'Yes. I know,' he replied rather smugly.

'It's also not very flattering Luiz,' said Celeste trying to be as subtle as she could. She did not want to be the one to dampen the fire of achievement; especially with Luiz, whom she thought a great deal of. Even though she was a *Sapphoist* and had no sexual interest in men. She'd often thought that he - having such a masculine name, Luiz Velázquez, being a tall, muscular, attractive Cuban dissident, Jazz saxophonist and motorcycle rider on the Wall of Death; whom had crashed several times which had left him with a small number of very manly scars that certain types of women find attractive and a devil-may-care attitude, was talented and interesting - that he would have appealed greatly and would have, had the circumstances been different, been a perfect lover.

'Well, it is not about fashion,' Luiz replied.

'It's probably just as well,' said Celeste.

Both Henri and Celeste then stared in silence.

Luiz looked from one to the other, then looked furtively around him. At that point, there was no one else on the terrace deck with them. He moved towards a door, took out a key from his pocket, opened it and went inside. A few moments later, he came out with a pair of long stepladders. He shut the door behind him and walked over to the safety railings. The next few moments seemed to play out in slow motion, yet with no time to comprehend what was happening. Luiz stepped on to the ladders and carefully walked tread by tread up to the top. This left him precariously balancing over the parapet. He then pulled on several tabs that were hidden in the trousers and under the shirt. Suddenly it became a one-piece ensemble; and expanded like a huge buoyancy aid, with two bat wing like flaps which extended from his waist to his wrists.

'I shall fly like a birdman Henri.' His statement of intent was followed by the animated laugh of a madman.

They both looked on in a silent, horrified, disbelief as he launched himself skywards.

The Cuban birdman, plummeted to earth like a boulder and although he bounced quite spectacularly several times, and *that*...was the end of Luiz Velázquez.

So then, I guess that goes a little way to presenting to you how my creative mind works. Although to be fair, that was the most surreal and otherworldly book I have written…so far that is.

I walked over to the taxi rank, got into the car at the front of the queue, and off we sped…or crawled actually, onward to the Eiffel Tower.

I paid the the driver, got out of the taxi and caught my first glimpse of the Tower. I have to say I was not disappointed. It looked absolutely wonderful. It's little wonder that, amongst his other ventures, Sir Edward Watkin tried to emulate Eiffel's Tower in Wembley Park, London, in 1892, unfortunately only getting to the height of 154 feet before running out of funding and disinterest from the locals and visitors alike. Although I had seen the Eiffel Tower many times in images and on film; what I was looking at, was just extraordinary.

It was still daylight, and sunset fell between 21:00 and 21:15, so I walked over to the little booking office, bought a timed ticket, and then I had a wander around the shops for a couple of hours or so. After which, I found a café – an expensive café, overlooking the Eiffel Tower.

I sat and sipped a glass of wine as the sun slipped away and dusk descended. The Tower became illuminated: even with the constant flow of traffic and people, I felt serene and content with all thoughts of the encounter in the park replaced by the scene that cinematically played out in front of me. It was seemingly, timeless.

It was time for me to go to the top of the Tower. As the elevator ascended, I thought about my crazy characters from the book making the same journey in another universe. I let out an involuntary girly giggle…there followed some strange looks from my fellow upwardly mobile passengers. As I said previously, novelists, have too much imagination. From the top, the view across Paris, even for an author, taxes the superlatives.

I wanted to cap off my seemingly very long and eventful day at Café de Paris V. I don't usually prescribe to repetition, but I'd had such a lovely evening there, that that's where I decided to go next.

Once again the jazz, the feel, the ambience and the sense of "cool" ended my day just right. I returned to my hotel…and bed.

The following morning, as my flight departure was at 11:15 from Charles de Gaulle, I had packed, had an early breakfast and was in a taxi nice and early as I had absolutely no idea just how long the journey might take.

After a smooth and uneventful 'check-in', I was sat in the spacious and well-organised departure lounge sipping a latte and going through the photos I had taken on my trip. As I scrolled through, a sense of dread came over me. Looking closely at the images, out of eight photos, the man from the gardens was in the background of five of them.

'*Shit!*'

I looked up apologetically, but luckily due to the size and space within the departure lounge there wasn't anyone in my immediate vicinity. I didn't know what to think? What did become clear to me, was that he *had* been following me; it was too much of a coincidence. But what did this mean exactly? Both of my scenarios still held water: he could have been in the hotel reception when I checked in, and in some wilfulness, decided to follow me. Or, could it be that the information he gave *was* true and that he was shadowing me; for what reason, I knew not? *Cui bono* – who benefits? If, what he claimed is true, why did he tell me there, in *that* place, and at *that* time, to disclose it to me? I know I have a colourful and creative imagination; but there he was, and I would be carrying him home with me in my photographs…my memories. In either scenario, in a purposeful predaciousness, he had become a part of my life…

CHAPTER FIVE

10:15 Friday 14ᵗʰ April 2023
Manchester Airport Departure lounge

It has been eleven months since I was last in Paris. So much has happened in that time.

After returning home, I put all thoughts of the interestingly weird encounter in the gardens behind me and chose instead, to remember the reason I went there; it had been such a pleasure and an honour, and I enjoyed Paris enormously. As I sit here now, I'm reflecting on how and why I find myself seated once more in a departure lounge, bound for Paris. On my return to my family home in Knutsford, I settled into my new novel and began the process of developing my characters and storyline. I can't speak for other novelists, and it's not always the case, but mostly the way it works for me is, I give life to those that are yet to exist. Then, the characters use me as the conduit and instrument of their thoughts and story telling. Now, I understand that it might sound a little strange; you expect a writer to sit, ponder and deliberate over each idea and instruct the protagonists of the where, what, why and when. The character led approach, is however, how it tends to run with me. I never really know what they are up to, or where they are going to take me next? There have been times I've started to write a book and its direction has changed beyond all recognition and plot. Where do the ides come from? Sometimes I could have the title and I might create the jacket for the book before the writing has even begun. That then gives me the impetuous and the spontaneity to "crack on" with it. Sometimes, it can come from a throw-away sentiment of a passing stranger, an overheard conversation in a café bar – you must have seen 'the writer' sitting in a café bar with their laptop open looking all interesting, meaningful and slightly bohemian – no, I don't do that, I just drink coffee. The idea could come from a whiff of scent, a line of a song or a life event. Turning these thoughts into creating a narrative that will stand up, fascinate, intrigue and compel the reader to continue to turn each page. That to me, is what writing is about.

As I just mentioned, another origin for a story, can come from a happening, or incident, as is the case with my new literary venture. So then, I began the story – with the help of my characters of course. The title of which is, Behind the Masque. It began its life set in 18ᵗʰ Century Venice. Although I have just said that I don't usually plan or overthink the plot, what I did do however with this novel, was to make a list of things that I wanted the story to include, offer and reveal to the reader:

Intrigue
Betrayal
Vengeance
An affair
Theft of idea
Hidden child's identity
Family deceptions
Stolen inheritance
Merchants
Incarceration
And a long kept secret.

All was going really well, until I needed to learn more about inheritance and genealogy. I'd asked Noah – my sister Chloe's partner who is a research academic of Medieval studies ("well that's handy you might say") to help me with my research.

Mainly I was reaching out for tips and shortcuts. Unwittingly however, the answers that had been thrown up by Noah, hurled me right back to the man in the gardens…

CHAPTER SIX

Thursday 10th November 2022
The Courtyard Coffee House,
Knutsford, Cheshire

We were sat at a table alfresco in the courtyard…

'Morning Noah.'
'Good morning Alice,' he replied looking rather bleary eyed.
He walked round the table to Chloe.
'Morning you,' he said passing her a warm smile. He bent over slightly and gave her a tender kiss on her cheek.
'Well that's nice,' she replied.
He pulled out a chair and sat down. He looked at us.

'Are you two having anything to eat?'

'Yes,' I said. Chloe smiled and nodded her head.

'Right then,' he said; his eyes now looking a little brighter. He picked up the menu.

The waitress came over to our table, and with an easy relaxed smile, she looked at us expectantly.

I returned the smile and nodded.

'Yes, I think we're good now.'

'I'll have eggs Benedict please, and a latte.'

Still smiling, the waitress turned and looked at Chloe.

'I'll have the same please, but gluten free and a latte also please,' said Chloe.

'Eggs Florentine for me please, and a cappuccino,' added Noah.

'Would you like your coffees now, or with your food?' enquired the waitress.

I looked at Chloe and Noah, and raised my eyebrows questioningly.

'Now?'

They both nodded.

'Sure,' said the waitress. 'I'll get them for you now.'

She turned and walked back into the café building.

'So?' said Noah looking at me curiously.

'So?' I replied.

'Yes. Genealogy. Why the sudden interest?'

'Oh. Yes, right. Well, I'm on with a new novel and…'

'Well done you,' he said.

I smiled.

'Yes. It's a little odd how it came about, but…'

'Odd?' enquired Chloe.

'Yes.'

Since my return from Paris, I hadn't discussed meeting the man in the park with anyone. Not through any sense of foreboding; I'd just put it on the back burner: forgotten about it really. I wanted to focus on the new book.

'How do you mean odd?' asked Noah.

'Well…getting the ideas for a new story can involve a little oddness here and there. This one was just that little bit stranger. But that's how it works sometimes.' I smiled and shrugged my shoulders as if it wasn't really that significant. I wanted to deflect any more questions about it to be honest as going back to the gardens in my mind, would be a distraction from my writing.

'So, to continue. For this new scribbling I need to know the process of tracing back ancestors. I thought you Noah, might just be the right man for the job.'

Noah beamed an impishly, half-cocked schoolboy grin.

'Well then, there you go.'

Chloe laughed.

'God Alice. Don't feed his intelligence.'

'You mean my modest, yet meticulousness intellect,' he said, grinning once again.

Alice punched him playfully in the arm…at least I think it was playfully.

'Don't get cocky.'

He beamed another smile.

'Just saying it as it is.'

'Yeah right.'

'Anyway,' I continued, 'Could you point me in the right direction Noah?'

'*Love to*. It'd be my pleasure.'

I nodded and smiled.

'Thanks. I appreciate it.'

He sat thoughtfully momentarily.

'If you want, I could use your own family tree to show you how to do the research?'

'Sounds good to me Noah.'

I don't know why but I felt a little apprehensive.

'When do you want to start?'

'Erm…'

'I could be around today. Unless…'

'Today would be good. Are you sure?'

He nodded.

'No problem.'

I thought for a moment.

'How about we throw a few things together and go to Tatton Park. We could make it a picnic this afternoon?'

I looked at them both.

'Oh I can't today Alice,' said Chloe. I've arranged to meet up with Georgia.'

'Oh OK.'

She continued, 'No reason why you two can't go?'

'I could come over to yours Alice,' said Noah.

Once again I sat in thought for a few moments...

'I don't really want mum and dad to know that I'm looking into the family history stuff.'

Chloe let out a small laugh.

'Why ever not?'

I shrugged my shoulders.

'I don't know why exactly. I erm...I don't know really.'

'I think you'll find that the first step on tracing your family tree...is your parents,' suggested Noah.

'Hmm. Yes. That would make sense.'

I sat and thought momentarily.

'I think I'm rushing ahead of myself a little. I'll speak to mum and dad and get the family background stuff and then we can take it from there. Maybe in a day or so. How does that sit with you Noah?'

He nodded.

'Yep. That would make sense. We can pick it up from where your folk's memories and family history goes back to. Family trees can be notoriously full of misinformation, half-truths and misleading stories.'

I narrowed my eyes in disbelief.

'Really?'

'Oh yes; sometimes not intentionally. For example, when Census records were taken, people had to submit their household information that was correct at that specific time. This was always on a Sunday night; the exact time of the Enumeration. That is, the Enumeration Officer asking the occupants to record that precise date and time. So, it could be for example, that staying in the house at that particular time was a friend, extended family member or lodger. Which could have implications for the interpretation of the data at a later time. The head of the household – usually the husband, unless he had died, or could have been elsewhere at that time, would not be present on the record and therefore, not living there. The same could be said of the children. A child could be in hospital or staying elsewhere with another relative that night. So, when future generations look at the Census record, it leaves it open to interpretation and questions. Why weren't the husband and father with his wife and children? Where was he? Where was the two-year-old child? Why was someone seemingly unrelated, staying at the house? You have to remember that whoever was on the Census record for that night, might not be the usual residents. They were just present at that one moment in time. Also, added to that: many people at the time of the early records, were innumerate and, or, illiterate or as the record was taken on trust, some people simply lied. So for instance, each subsequent Census, could give them a different age. The lack of accuracy or misinformation, could be an honest error, or intentional.'

'Intentional?' queried Chloe.

'Yes. Occasionally, the occupants didn't want to reveal the correct information or dates, as it might raise questions.'

'What kinds of questions?' I asked.

'Well, origin of birth, immigration, their age, as it could have had implications for certain types of work they were doing, or even how old the mother was at the birth of a child. If you look deeper and obtain birth, marriage or death certificates, you quite often find contradictory information. Names are changed or added to occupations and age. Remember, that the Enumeration officers for the census and Registrars at that time didn't question the given information. Most of the time, the person registering the birth, marriage etc. didn't have certificates to verify the information. A lot of the time in the older records, it was given verbally, and written down accordingly.'

I was slightly taken aback. I hadn't really given any thought to family history in depth before. What Noah was telling me, actually got me quite excited.

'You say that they sometimes changed names on certificates,' questioned Chloe. 'Why?'

Noah laughed. He looked at us both and smiled broadly.

'For reasons that might suit a particular purpose. It can be an absolute minefield!'

I sat back in my chair; now fired up to discover my own family tree, and with thoughts flying around wildly about my book, Behind the Masque. Then, another darker thought entered my mind. "You are not who you think yourself to be Alice". Is it possible that there might be some concealment; either unintentional or surreptitiously, in *my* family tree. Now my blood was really up.

'I'll speak to mum and dad tonight Noah.'

He smiled.

'Happy journey.'

'I hope so,' I said impishly.

Chloe laughed.

'What do you mean by that?'

'Well…who knows?'

57

As yet, I wasn't ready yet to reveal the purpose anyone, which had now changed from researching for a book, to a more personal and intimate search...

CHAPTER SEVEN

Later that evening, at home, Knutsford

'I'll have a look for you Alice.'

'Thanks dad. I really appreciate it.'

My mum was walking through the lounge.

'What's prompted a sudden desire to look at your ancestry?' She asked.

'It's for a new novel.'

'Oh how lovely.'

Then a look of slight puzzlement.

'It's not about our family is it Alice?'

I laughed.

'No Mum. It's set in Venice in the middle-ages and I need a better understanding of how family history is uncovered.'

My mum continued, 'Sounds fascinating darling.'

'Noah is going to help me.'

'Yes, I could see where his knowledge might be useful,' said my dad. My dad sat thoughtfully momentarily.

'Where did the idea come from Alice?'

I answered with care.

'Where do they *ever* come from dad? You tell me? I haven't a clue!'

I smiled. Mum laughed. Dad looked strangely mystified.

Mum stroked her chin.

'I expect they'll all be together in the family trunk in the attic, won't they Andrew?'

'What?' he replied with a look surprise.

'The family documents…you know…'

'Oh. Yes. Yes. I'll have a look tomorrow for you Alice.'

'Could I possibly look at them now dad. If that's OK…if there is nothing private or secretive in there that you might not want me rummaging through.'

Mum laughed and looked at dad.

'*No!* Certainly nothing secret in there Alice. I'm sure of that.'

Dad seemed a little more hesitant.

'Dad?'

'No. I mean, yes. Of course you can Alice. Do you know where it is?'

I was a little puzzled having just established where they were.

'Yes dad. In the attic.'

He nodded.

'Yes. Just…well be careful. There's a lot of old papers in there. Some are irreplaceable.'

'Sure dad. I'll be careful. Thanks.'

I went through to the hallway, and up the three flights of stairs to the attic, which had undergone a loft conversion to become a study. I kneeled down and slowly slid out the trunk containing the family stuff. I had never looked in it before; I guess family "stuff" had never really interested me before now. Now however, I was *really* interested. Gingerly, I began to remove the contents and placed them on a work desk that we sometimes used if we wanted to escape the rest of the family. There were all sorts of papers and documents including birth, baptism, marriage and death notices. Some seemed a lot older than others.

I made a separate pile of relevant papers and documents relating to our family tree that I thought might be of use. There were no Census records, but at least I had names on certificates that I felt sure Noah would find useful to begin the journey backwards. There was also an envelope that had written on it, Obituary. I don't know why I didn't open it there and then. I thought that it might be best to pass it all on to Noah to look at. There were a few newspaper sheets and a bunch of documents bound together in a leather binding. They looked really old. I picked up my mobile as Chloe walked into the attic.

'Oh family rummaging's eh. You never know what skeletons you may unearth.'

I stared at her. She couldn't possibly know the reason for my "rummaging" of course. But her sentiment sent a shiver down my spine and set off a wave of goose bumps.

She smiled.

'Are you OK Alice?'

I gave an affected laugh.

'Yes; of course. I'm just looking forward to starting my new novel. When I set sail with a new scribbling, my head tends not to be in the room, if you know what I mean.'

She laughed.

'No! But I'll take your word for it.'

I smiled.

'Yep. It's an odd thing sure enough.'

'So, have you found anything interesting yet?'

'No. Not yet. I'm just gathering together what I think might be useful for Noah.'

'He's really fired up about it Alice.'

I was a little taken aback.

'Really.'

'Absolutely up his street. He loves looking at people's family trees. He's really good at it. He's found information for, and about people of which they had no idea.'

'Hmm.'

I picked up my mobile.

'Hi Noah,' I looked at Chloe's face. She was beaming a smile. 'Are you free tomorrow?' I put him on loudspeaker.

'Have you found something?'

'Yes. Well, not found anything exactly, I've just got together a few birth, death and marriage certificates and some other papers.'

'Cool. I could pop round about two o'clock tomorrow afternoon. How does that sound?'

I knew mum was having friends over tomorrow afternoon. The weather was going to be promising, so, 'how about we meet at the Courtyard Coffee House and then maybe Tatton Park?'

'Sounds good to me. Are you coming along Chloe?'

Chloe leaned forward to speak but Noah continued,' I've just remembered that you've got a Ward round tomorrow haven't you.'

She laughed.

'Well remembered you.'

He returned a laugh.

'You see. I do listen.'

'Two O'clock then Noah,' I said.

'Absolutely. Can't wait.'

'Really.'

'You see. I told you,' said Chloe.

'See you then. And thanks Noah. I really appreciate it.'

'My pleasure. See you then. Night Chloe.'

'Good night you. See you tomorrow evening.'

'Absolutely. Can't wait.'

'Cheeky bugger,' replied Chloe impishly.

I ended the call and placed my phone on top of the family letters and documents. I looked at them and then to Chloe. I smiled.

'Right then.'

She laughed.

'I've got an early start Alice. I'm going to turn in.'

'OK. Good night Chloe.'

She smiled broadly.

'Good night Alice. You're all excited aren't you.'

I returned a giddy schoolgirl shake of the head and beamed a smile.

'You *bet* I am. I can't wait to see where this takes me.'

She smiled once again.

'Night then. Enjoy the journey.'

'Night Chloe. And thanks.'

She looked a little puzzled.

'Thanks? Thanks for what?'

'Just…just for being you.'

She narrowed her eyes and gave me a wry smile.

'Erm. OK then.' She turned and waved her right hand in the air.

'Night then.'

I smiled affectionately. I couldn't have wished for a better sister than Chloe. She means the world to me.

I picked up the pile of paperwork I had put together and carried it downstairs and through to the lounge.

Both mum and dad were sat there.

'Any luck?' asked mum.

I shrugged my shoulders.

'Oh. Early days yet.'

'My dad stared at the pile of material I'd gathered together. Then to me. It was a strange inquisitive look.

'You OK dad?'

'He seemed a little startled.

'Oh. Yes. I'm fine.'

'Right.'

I smiled.

'Are you sure it's OK for me to go through this stuff dad?'

'Of course it is Alice.'

'OK. Just going to get my laptop.'

I placed the pile on the sofa next to my dad. He stared expressionlessly at them.

I turned and went upstairs to my room. I picked up the laptop, left the room and walked back down to the lounge.

I smiled at my dad.

'Are either of you using the conservatory?'

Both shook their heads.

'Fab.'

I picked up the letters and documents etc. walked out of the lounge, across the hallway and into the conservatory. I shut the door behind me, placed the laptop and documents on the tabletop, withdrew a chair and sat down. I opened up my laptop, switched it on and then opened a new folder: Behind the Masque (history stuff). I opened a new word document, saved it as family history, then I placed the new folder into the folder I had already created for the new novel: Behind the Masque. I looked out through the conservatory windows across the meadow, to the woodland in the distance. I closed my lips; breathed in a deep breath through my nostrils, opened my mouth and let it out slowly through my mouth. I smiled contentedly.

'Right then.'

I moved my laptop to one side and slid the documents in front of me.

After a quick rummage through the material; I had separated the birth, marriage and death certificates from the rest of the additional paperwork, which I placed to one side.

After about half-an-hour or so of reading through the certificates, which I found fascinating and informative; it all seemed pretty straightforward to me. I opened up my computer, then the folder and new word document and began to add the dates and family members into it.

It had turned midnight and I was feeling rather tired so I turned in for the night. I had begun the journey with enthusiasm and innocence, and as it was being revealed to me, a kind of familiarity and comfort set over me. Maybe I was being a little naïve and trusting of this new clarification and understanding of who I am, and where I have come from. The answers lay in the future; yet to be discovered and revealed…

CHAPTER EIGHT

14:13
Friday 11th November 2022.
The Courtyard Coffee House,
Knutsford, Cheshire

'Hi Noah. Sorry I'm a little late.'

'Hi Alice. That's OK. Just got here myself.'

'I see. So, you were late for me then!'

He laughed.

'Erm. Well…not really,'

I smiled, leaned across the table and gave him a kiss on his cheek. I placed my laptop on the table and messenger bag on the floor next to my chair, and sat down. He looked at my bag and smiled.

I nodded my head.

'Oh Yeah,' I said, self-confidently.

He laughed.

'Coffee?'

I smiled.

'Coffee would be just great.'

He had just raised his head as the same waitress from the day before came over to the table.

'Hello again,' she said with a warm smile.

'Hi,' we both said in unison.

Noah looked at me.

'Latte?'

I nodded.

'A Cappuccino and a Latte please.'

'Of course. Would you like a sprinkling of chocolate on the cappuccino?'

'Oh. No thank you.'

'Thank you,' said the waitress as she turned and headed back inside the café.

Noah looked at me, settled back in his chair and smiled.

'Well?'

'Well what?' I said returning a cheeky grin.

'You know very well what.'

'Luckily for me, my mum and dad...although I didn't ask and I'm guessing more my dad, has collected family documents certificates etc. together. It's made it a little easier for me.'

I opened up the laptop, as Noah shifted his chair closer to me to gain a better view.

I opened the folder and then the Word document. He began to scrutinise the information that it contained.

'Behind the Masque,' he said. 'Nice title by the way. Care to reveal?'

'Not a chance,' I said, grinning like a Cheshire cat.

After a few minutes…

'Well that all seems fairly straightforward to me so far. No skeletons there then.'

'So far?'

'A long and winding road, is genealogy Alice. What's in the bag?'

'Some other papers. Some seem quite a bit older than others…to me at least.'

'Now I'm *really* interested.'

The waitress came over to the table carrying the coffees on a small tray. She placed the latte next to me and the cappuccino next to Noah, followed by a small plate of assorted biscuits.

'Complimentary,' she said, as she gave us both another warm smile. 'Can I get you anything else?'

We both smiled.

'Not for me thank you,' I said.

Noah smiled and shook his head.

'OK. Enjoy.' She walked back over to the Coffee House.

I bent down and removed some of the contents from my bag.

'I've separated the documents and letters etc. into what *I* think are related.'

I passed him a small bundle wrapped in a rubber band.

'It was late when I was going through these, and I was a little tired, so, they may or may not be relevant.'

He moved his chair back to its original position, and took a sip of coffee.

'Ahh. That's hit the spot.'

I followed suit.

'Amen to that.'

He placed his cup back into its saucer and picked up the small bundle. He removed the rubber band and sat back into his chair.

Unspoken, one by one he analysed the documentation. He was so absorbed that he seemed oblivious to his surroundings and me. He was completely lost. I sat and sipped my coffee in silence. It was wonderful seeing him work. I had never seen him portray that sort of intensity before. This was a very different Noah that I was observing.

71

After what seemed an age, he looked down at the bag, and then to me.

'Is there more in the bag?'

I nodded.

'Yes.'

'Could I see the word document again?'

Once again I nodded.

'Sure. Have you found something?'

He shrugged his shoulders.

'Maybe.'

I opened the document and turned it around to face him. He looked at it and then turned it back round.

'Can I look at the other stuff?'

'Of course you can. That's why I brought it.'

He smiled.

'I'm so glad you did.'

I laughed.

'I can see that.'

He looked a little perplexed.

'How do you mean?'

'Well Noah. You're sat in a café with a stunningly attractive and intelligent young woman, and you haven't noticed me in, well, minutes.'

He narrowed his eyes and then let out a hearty laugh.

'I'm sorry. For a moment there, I thought you were talking about someone else.'

'Cheeky bugger.'

He laughed again.

'What is it with you and your sister calling me a cheeky bugger. A man could take offence.'

'I'd take the advice if I were you.'

'Fair point.'

I lifted up the bag and passed it over to him.

'There is nothing you wouldn't want me to see in that bag is there?'

'You mean like incriminating photographs?'

Once again he narrowed his eyes before the recognition of a hint of sarcasm.

'Very good.'

He opened the flap and removed the rest of the contents. He looked at me.

'I know. You're going to disappear again.'

He smiled.

I watched him once again as he studied and clinically dissected the information that was now spread across the table.

After a short while he looked up from the paperwork at me.

'Hmm.'

He looked down once again.

'What? What does that mean; "Hmm"? *Have* you found something?'

He looked at me again.

He gave me a narrowed eyed, furrowed browed hesitant kind of expression.

'I'm not sure. I'd like to take this with me. Do you think that would be OK with your mum and dad?'

'Yeah. I can't see that being a problem. What is it you think you might have found?'

'I didn't say I'd found *anything*,' he said smiling. 'I said, I'm not sure.'

'OK then Mr academic. If you're not sure, that implies that there is a possibility that there is something.'

'Hmm.'

'Oh don't give me the "Hmm" again.'

He laughed.

'Honestly Alice; it would be wrong of me to second-guess. It could mislead you. Remember what I said about tracing family history…minefield. You have to have good empirical evidence. I'll have to do some digging…but yes; I think there may be something that's not sitting quite right.'

'Will you let me know as soon as.'

'Of course I will. Then we can sit down together and you'll be able to see how the process works. It will give you clues and the best approach for researching your book: which is what the whole exercise is about, really. There's always something new to discover in everyone's family tree Alice. It wouldn't be unusual if I did uncover something in yours. In fact, I'd be surprised if there wasn't a skeleton or two.'

I couldn't make out whether he had already found something and that he was pacifying me temporarily; or that he had spotted the possibility of a skeleton. I guess I would have to wait and see.

We finished our coffee and with kisses on cheeks and a hug, we parted.

Over the next few days, I felt that I couldn't proceed with my book. I was in a kind of literary limbo. I needed to know how to go about researching family trees to be able to give a sense of direction to the plotline. Added to that though, I couldn't focus on the narrative if I had tried. Noah's noncommittal caution had created a sort of shroud over the book. As it transpired, he was right to have been cautious; as I was once again, as in the *Jardin des Plantes*, in Paris, caught out by my naivety…

CHAPTER NINE

Monday 14th November 2022.
09:37
Knutsford, Cheshire

I was walking down King Street, when my mobile rang out. It was Noah.

'Hi Noah. How are things?'

'Hi Alice. Good yes. Very good. How are you?'

'All good thanks. You've not been around the last few days.'

'As you know, Chloe's been on night shift at A&E, so…'

'Oh yes. You're right. Sorry I forgot.'

There was a slight pause before he continued, 'I think I have found something?'

I was thrilled, but puzzled. I laughed.

'You *think*? I thought you had to have empirical evidence before you committed.'

I heard him let out a small sigh.

'Yes you're right. Something isn't sitting quite right and I thought I'd let you know as it's been a few days without contacting you.'

'I'm intrigued.'

'Yes. So am I. Are you at home at the moment?'

'No. But I can be within about fifteen minutes.'

There followed a short silence…

'Noah?'

'Yes. Sorry I'm here.'

'You're being a bit cagey.'

'Are your folks at home Alice? I'm sure Chloe said that they were away for a couple of days?'

'Oh yes,' I said, suggestively, 'And what have you got in mind then? Remember, I share *everything* with my sister.'

'What?'

'Oh never mind. This conversation is becoming a bit of a drama if I'm honest. Just drop by. I'll be at home shortly and I'll meet you there.'

'OK. That's a plan.'

'Later.'

'Bye Alice.'

I laughed. The woman I was walking past at the time, didn't seem to share my random sense of humour.

It was 10:23 when the front door bell rang.

'Hello you.'

'Hello Alice. How are you?'

'Intrigued.'

He laughed.

'Yes you said that earlier.'

'Come in.'

We went though to the lounge.

'Coffee?'

'Love one.'

I went off to the kitchen and made two coffees. I walked back into the lounge and placed Noah's coffee in front of him on the table. As I sat down I noticed that he had my messenger bag with him.

'Been rummaging then?'

'Pardon?' I looked down at my bag by his side and nodded my head.

'*Oh*! Yes. Rummaging. Good word. Appropriate.'

'So, then?'

He bent down; removed a few documents and other pieces of paper that I didn't recognise. He spread them out across the table but he seemed to be placing them in some kind of order or sequence.

He picked up his coffee, took a sip, sat back into the sofa and then stared at the table.

I coughed affectedly.

78

'Well?'

'Right then. I've printed off some material that should help you to discover two things: one, how to go about carefully researching a family tree in support of your new novel, Behind the Masque.'

I smiled broadly.

'Well remembered.'

'You're welcome. Two…' he hesitated. 'Your own family tree.'

'OK. Let's get started.'

Looking through the documentation you gave me; I think that you had already an idea of your recent family history. Looking at your paternal side: Your dad, Andrew Garner, born 1970 in Cheshire, age fifty-three. And his father, your Grandfather, Thomas Garner, born in Shropshire in 1937 and died in 2008. Your mother's side is fairly well detailed also. But it's your Father's line that is…' he paused momentarily, then smiled impishly, 'Intriguing.'

I stood up and sat next to him on the sofa.

'Continue,' I said with a smile.'

'OK. So, not all, but most people have knowledge of their immediate family history: father, mother grandparents, cousins, aunts and uncles etc. Including in many cases, Godparents. However, at some point the information becomes less and a little cloudier. That's when we reach out to the Census records for the next step in the search. Incidentally, the Venetians kept meticulous records. I just thought I'd mention that. You know, for your book.'

'Yes I got that Noah,' I said with a playful smile and an unsubtle hint of sarcasm.

'Right then. So, the UK Census records are available for the years 1841 to 1921 and were taken every ten years. The 1931 Census records were destroyed in a fire in 1942. There is a hundred years gap between the release of the Census due to not offending, or releasing information about any individual that could still be alive today.'

'Some people live beyond a hundred.'

'This is true. However, when it was first decided to wait a hundred years before releasing the data, people generally, didn't survive beyond a hundred. So, that was the safety net.'

I nodded.

'OK. Got that.

Once again he hesitated before continuing.

'So. Without 'bigging' myself up, due to my empirical research in medieval studies, the university has given me privileged access to fast-track Census records. The next person I wanted to find was your Great Grandfather. Do you know anything about him?'

I shook my head.

'No. Nothing. In fact, I know hardly anything about my grandfather let alone, my great grandfather. From what you just said, my dad was only nine years old when his dad, my grandfather died. I'm guessing he didn't know too much about his own father.'

'I found your Great Grandfather, George Garner, on the 1911 Census.' He reached across to the first sheet of paper in line. He handed it to me.

I looked at it and as I hadn't seen one before, I looked at him for a little help.

'OK. What you're looking at is quite a detailed record of who was in a particular residence on the Enumeration date.' Do you remember me explaining about how and when the Census was taken?'

I nodded.

'Yes. I remember that.'

'OK. So...' he took out a pen from his pocket and pointed it at the first column. 'These are the addresses of the residences, street, road, number etc. Next to it are the names of the people in each individual property - not necessarily living there remember, but there that evening. Then, their ages and gender. OK.'

I nodded.

He passed it over to me.

I scrutinised the Census. Then I found him.

'*There!*'

He looked at the Census.

'Where?'

I pointed.

'There. I see him. George Garner - son - aged 2.' I looked at the names above. 'Head of household – Clarice Garner - age 27. George had a brother, Laurie - age 4 and a sister - Suzanne - age 6. *Wow!* I've just met my Great Grandfather!' I beamed a self-satisfied smile and placed it on to the tabletop. He smiled.

'OK. Were there any other documents in the trunk that looked like they could be related to George?'

I thought for a moment.

'I don't think so,' I replied with a little hesitancy.

'Hmm. I wouldn't mind having a look through them. Do you think that would be OK with your folks?'

'I don't see why not. I did tell them that you were helping me. Why are you interested in George?'

'It's not George that I'm interested in. I'll explain.' He picked up the Census record. 'This is the 1911 Census. As George's father wasn't on that Census as, Head of household, he had to be somewhere at that time. Unless, he had died, been hospitalised, in the Military or left the country, or…didn't want to be found.' He looked at me impassively.

I was a little mystified.

'Go on Noah. Tell me what you've found.'

He smiled and continued, 'the best way forward was to find a birth record for George. As it wasn't in the pile of stuff you gave me, I presumed it wasn't amongst the other paperwork in the trunk.'

I shook my head.

'I don't recall seeing a birth certificate for a George Garner.'

'So, I contacted my friend at the Records Office. George's Father was a Henry Garner, born 1882, in London. So then, I had enough information to look for him in the 1891 Census. I found him.'

He moved to a sheet of paper that was next in line and passed to me. I read it out, 'Henry Garner - age 11. Head of Household - Louis Garner - age 34. Yevette Garner - wife - age 32. He had two sisters: Yevette – age 10 and Céleste – age 14. *Yay!* Another ancestor. I'm beginning to like this Noah.'

Once again the impassive expression set across his face. Then he let out a sigh.

I shrugged my shoulders.

'What? What does that mean?'

'Now I had definitive evidence for Henry, his parents and his siblings, it should have been an easy next step backwards. I checked the 1881 Census Records. They were nowhere to be found.'

I thought for a moment.

'In 1881, Henry would have been age 1, Yevette, age 2 and Céleste, age 4. They should be together on the same record…shouldn't they?'

'Remember what I said, that occasionally, some of the residents were not at that address on the Census night for whatever reason. But for all of the family to be absent, but present in the next Census led me down another path. This path kept me up all night!' He smiled affectionately. 'But it was worth it.'

I sat there mesmerised. He continued, 'there was an envelope, an old envelope that hadn't, as far as I could see, had ever been opened.'

'The one with Obituary written on it?'

'Yes. That one.' He sat in thought, momentarily before continuing, 'do you know of any French blood in your family?'

My heart was wildly palpitating; so much so, that I thought he would see it through my top. The statement, "you are not who you think yourself to be Alice" came back to my mind, in very large font! *'Shit!'*

'Are you OK Alice?'

'Yes. It's erm…nothing. I'm fine.'

'Are you sure. You went really pale just then.'

I forced a smile.

'No. Honestly. I'm fine Noah. Carry on please.'

He's no fool and he could tell that there *was* something. He continued once again, 'the letter is a tribute to a Louis Rochambeau of Clichy, France. It's not really what the tribute is about that's interesting, it's that Louis Rochambeau and Louis Garner are one and the same person.'

'What?' I said in bewilderment.

'It took me a while, but to cut a long story short; the tribute mentioned his wife, Yevette Rochambeau, formally, Yvette Garnier, pronounced Gar-nee-yay. The nearest equivalent in English is Garner.'

'They changed their names.'

He nodded.

'Yes. They did. It seems to tie in with their move from France to England. It seems he took her maiden name and rebranded if you like, the family.'

I found a French document stating that Louis Rochambeau and his wife, Yvette were living in the Dordogne region, with his children: Céleste, Henry and Yvette in 1884. For some reason Alice, your family changed their country and their name. And at this point, I have no idea why? I have written a brief summary of dates for you.' He slid the next paper in line on the table, over to me.

Andrew Garner – Father - born 1970. Cheshire

Thomas Garner - Grandfather – born 1937.
Shropshire.

George Garner – Great Grandfather – born 1909.
Shropshire.

Henry Garner – G G Grandfather – born 1882.
London.

Louis Rochambeau – G G Grandfather X 2 – 1857.
Clichy. France.
Wife – Yevette Garnier (Gar-nee-yay)
Children:
Yevette – born 1881
Henry – born 1882
Céleste – born 1884

My mind was in a whirl. The meeting in the garden
in Paris; now had some meaning to it, and a greater
significance. But what did it actually mean? And
why was someone, some *stranger*, reminding me of
a past, that I never knew I had. At that moment in
time, all thoughts of Medieval Venice, left the
building. There it was then; a French connection. It

didn't feel like closure in any sense; it felt like I was just at the beginning of something significant…

CHAPTER TEN

Tuesday 22nd November 2022.
10:21
Courtyard Coffee House,
Knutsford, Cheshire

After disclosing to me at my home, what he had found, Noah had spent the rest of the day on his own in the attic going through everything in the trunk, in the hope of finding some clues as to what it all means. I still hadn't told him, or anyone come to that, about the man in the gardens and what he had said to me. I wanted to hold back that information for the present. To Noah of course, this family history search was nothing more than a teaching aid to help me in my research for my new novel; he had no way of knowing the significance and implications that he had, and was in the process of uncovering.

I had seen Noah on and off over the past few days as he came for Chloe; but nothing was mentioned about his research into my family...and as he wasn't saying...I wasn't asking.

I had a missed call from Noah asking if we could meet up again to discuss my family tree. The presumption was, that he had discovered something else. I called him back and arranged to meet at the Courtyard Coffee House.

'Hi Noah.'
'Hi Alice. You OK?'
I smiled.
'All good thanks. And you?'
'Tickety-boo.'
I laughed.
He shrugged his shoulders.
'What?'
'Do people still say that?'
'Well I do.'
I smiled.
'Well OK then. I saw you drive past when I was walking up. I've ordered the coffee's.'
'Cool. Thanks.'

'Would you rather sit inside?'

He shook his head.

'No. It's a little chilly, but such a lovely morning. Unless…'

'No. I'm good here.'

'OK then.'

'So.'

'Hmm.'

'There it is again.'

'What?'

'Whenever something is coming at me, it starts with a "Hmm".'

He laughed.

'Yeah. I do do that don't I.'

'Yes you do. Well?'

'So.

'I know that the idea of this exercise was to help you to understand how to go about researching a family tree to help you with your book. But; this has become so absorbing that I feel that I have taken my eye off the ball.'

'How do you mean?'

'Well…'

'Two coffee's,' interjected the chirpy waitress.

'Oh thanks so much,' I said offering her a warm smile.

'You're welcome. Would there be anything else?'

I looked at Noah. We both shook our heads.

'Not at the moments thanks,' I said.

'OK. Just let me know.' She turned smartly and went back inside.

'Eye off the ball Noah?'

'Yes. So, I feel that I'm getting into this a little too much and not really explaining the process. Most of the research I'm doing is on my own, which is not showing you how it's done. Not helping I guess.'

He didn't know just how hungry I was for more revelations.

'I absolutely don't mind. My novel aside, I'm loving what you are discovering about my family.'

'Really!'

I laughed.

'Yes. Really.'

'Oh. OK then,' he let out a sigh and then gave a broad smile. 'That's great. It's becoming really interesting.'

My heart began to race.

'So. Have you discovered something more?'

He nodded.

'Yes. I think I have found something. I tried to trace your paternal line - Louis Rochambeau your Great Great Grandfather times 2, but I hit a wall. They had vanished...no trace. But I dug a little deeper and began to think like him.'

'Think like him?'

'Yes. I thought that if they changed their name once, they could quite possibly have changed it before. I'm waiting on some documents from a French colleague, but what I managed to find did show that they seemed to change name regularly; often tying in with a move to another place.'

'So, they change their family names each time they move to someplace else.'

He looked a little puzzled.

'That's what I just said.'

I laughed.

'Sorry Noah. I was being a bit blonde there.'

His eyes widened.

'Are you even allowed to say that anymore?'

'It may have escaped your attention; but I am blonde.'

'Well, I would say, mousey.'

'It's flaxen…blonde.'

He held up his hands in submission.

'OK OK. Blonde it is.'

I smiled and nodded with confidence.

'Well alright then.'

He smiled and then took a sip of coffee.

'That's good.'

'Louis Rochambeau?'

'Oh yes. As I said I'm waiting for my colleague to get back to me. He's as geeky as I am when it comes to tracing historical stuff; especially the Medieval.'

'Medieval? You think we go back that far?'

He smiled.

'Well…you're sat here. So, your bloodline must go back to the Stone Age and beyond. It's a miracle really if you think about it. Our bloodlines have survived everything that's been thrown at them: The Ice age, famine, wars, plagues, diseases, the incessant hard toil of the Industrial revolution and the Conservative Party.'

I laughed.

'I thought you were a Conservative?'

'I…really don't know anymore to be honest. They all seem to promise mountains and deliver molehills. Politics – Poli (many) tics (blood sucking insects).'

I laughed once again, but a little more raucously. Noah raised his eyebrows and followed suit.

We both settled down and drank a little coffee. Noah placed his cup back in his saucer and thoughtfully moved it around. I knew he had something more to say about his findings. I let him have a little space.

He looked up at me.

'I have found something a little nearer to home Alice. And, if I'm right'…he hesitated, 'it could well be a novel in itself.'

I leaned forward on to my elbows.

'When you say nearer to home, do you mean time wise; as in, not the Middle-ages?'

He nodded.

'Yes. The nineteen-sixties. Again, on your dad's side.'

I tried to remember which forebear that would be.

'Thomas?'

'Yes Thomas Garner born 1937.'

'What happened? What have you found?'

'Believe me when I say that I was up day and night with this. It took some unravelling and is very complex. I have just one more thing to verify though before I tell you. I want to make absolutely sure that what I reveal to you is what really happened.'

I felt a little disappointed, yet at the same time, so wrapped with excitement.

'When do you think you'll know?'

'I have a few lectures to facilitate over the next couple of days. But, I would say…' he sat thoughtfully briefly. 'I would say Sunday.'

'My folks are off to the holiday home in Dartmouth on Saturday for a week.'

'I could pop round.'

I laughed.

'What?'

'Chloe will be getting suspicious about us. I'm seeing more of you than she is.'

'Actually, you're wrong. I've been telling her about your family tree and she's fascinated. In fact, I'd like her to be there if she isn't on duty at A&E.'

'She didn't say that you had told her.'

He laughed.

'She wasn't sure whether you would want her to know?'

I shook my head.

'Of *course* I do. It's Chloe's family as much as mine.'

He laughed.

'Well, that's all right then.'

I looked at him. I like Noah; he's a really sound bloke. He's honest, attentive, funny, intelligent, caring and he is so kind to Chloe...and me for that matter.

'How are things with you two?'

He sat back into his chair.

'Things are just tickety-boo.'

We both laughed.

'You are so good together Noah. I'm so happy for you both.'

'I'm that lucky guy you read about in romance novels.'

'You read romance novels?'

He shook his head.

'No.' he replied nonchalantly.

I smiled affectionately.

'I really appreciate what you're doing for me Noah. It's really good of you.'

'Hey. My pleasure. Actually I'm being a little self-serving.'

I narrowed my eyes.

'I doubt you could ever be that. How do you mean?'

'I'm just after a credit in the acknowledgments of, Behind the Masque.'

'It's a deal,' I said, followed by a hearty laugh.

We finished off our coffees and went on our way. Me, to a friend's house in Plumley and as Chloe's car was in for an MOT, Noah went off to pick up Chloe from the hospital.

I don't know exactly just what I was expecting in the next chapter of my family's story. Even though I write and create fiction; I could not have imagined what was to be revealed to me next...

CHAPTER ELEVEN

Sunday 27th November 2022.
11:30
At home in Knutsford.

The doorbell rang…

'I'll get it,' shouted Chloe from the kitchen. 'It'll be Noah.'

I was sat in the lounge when the door opened.

I smiled.

'Hi Noah.'

I stood up and he leaned forward to kiss me on my cheek.

'How are you Alice?'

'I'm good thanks. And you?'

He smiled warmly.

'Yes. I'm good thanks.'

I noticed he had with him, a leather bag. I gave him an animated smile and couldn't disguise the fact that I was a little enthusiastic to hear what he had discovered. He looked at me, smiled and nodded his head.

The door opened and Chloe walked backwards into the room carrying a tray.

'I've made a cafetiere, if that fits with everyone?'

She placed it on the table, then the mugs and a large serving plate of cheeses, grapes, chopped apple and various biscuits. We looked at her. She smiled.

'A few mid-morning nibbles, always go down well...don't you think.'

During the week, I had talked to Chloe about the research into our family history. Noah was right, she was as keen as I to hear more.

The coffees poured I sat waiting for what news he had found.

Noah bent down unzipped his bag and took out a few documents. As before, he seemed to set them out in a particular order.

He picked up one of the sheets of paper and sat back into the sofa.

'OK then. I think I have found something.'

'Wow. How exciting,' said Chloe.

He looked directly at me.

'However, as I hinted at last time, it isn't, or on the face of it, doesn't seem to be related to the distant past. The first piece of information relates to your Grandfather, Thomas Garner born 1937.' He stopped momentarily and looked at Chloe.

'It's OK Noah,' said Chloe, 'Alice's brought me up to speed. She showed me the genealogy you've discovered so far.'

He smiled, leaned forward, picked up his mug, took a sip of coffee, placed it back onto the table and sat once again back into the sofa. He looked from me to Chloe then back again before continuing, 'I still have work to do on this particular story and at the moment, I'm not to sure as to how I'm going to proceed. It would appear that Thomas was, for the want of a better word, mixed up with the communist movement here in the UK during the nineteen-sixties and maybe beyond. Not just in a spectator come follower kind of way, but an earnest involvement. He was actively promoting and recruiting for the Communist party. However, it is his father, your Great Grandfather, George Garner born 1909, who would be age thirty in 1939 that I think you will find to be more interesting. I certainly do.'

'Yes. That's what it said on the Census. But, I'm not so sure that that was truthful. In March 1944, George is in France.

'France? I was a little puzzled. 'The war was still on-going in 1944 wasn't it?'

'Yes. But he was there, in France. It also seems that he, as with your Grandfather, had sympathies and inclinations towards the left...the communists. At that time, though he had kept it secret.'

He breathed in deeply then released a sigh.

'OK. Let me wind it back a little. It's more complex than this, but simply put: During World War Two, after France capitulated or surrendered, in nineteen-forty, France signed an Armistice agreement where the country was essentially divided into two areas; North and South. German Occupied regions which included, northern France and all of the Atlantic coastline down the border of Spain. And in the south, a self-governing and supposedly neutral region, called Vichy was established. It was run by the French, but under German supervision and with their co-operation. During this time of occupation and the Vichy; there were those that went along with the armistice, either through fear, or they didn't object to either the occupation or Vichy, but there were others, the majority, who were against German rule. The resistance could be described as haphazard and involved various factions or Cells.

Communication between them was quite poor and some times, non-existent. Occasionally, it was more serious where there were many deceptions. Politics drove the various resistance groups, and as now, politics can be a dirty and deceitful business. Although having the same reason as the other factions of resistance, that is, fighting to free France from the subjugation by the Germans, the communists were not always welcomed. Many of the French were suspicious about the ideology of Communism, and looked towards France post collaboration and occupation. They were afraid that after the war, the Communists would have too much power and were in some cases, despised as much as the Germans. How much of that is a reality and would have happened...the jury is still out. Even now, rumours and stories from that time still come to the surface to be debated, denied or accepted. We might never know. However, back to George. I've told you a little about the undercurrent within the resistance. In 1944 the D-Day landings took place. Do you know what I mean by the D-Day landings, the allies landed in France, that is: The British, Americans, Free French and many other nationalities that were at War with Germany.'

'Yes. I do,' I said.

'Me too,' said Chloe.

'So. Prior to the landings, as you can imagine, there was an incredible amount of careful planning involved. This planning included deceptions by the Allies. What I mean by that is, purposely leaked documents, disinformation and propaganda in order to give the Germans false trails. The Germans knew the invasion was going to happen; they just didn't know where or when. So various intricate and top-secret deception plans were put in place by the Allies to confuse them. Over in France, the resistance really stepped up their sabotage and disruption. The British had secret agents, many of whom belonged to a department called the Special Operations Executive, or SOE. There were other British agencies including the Special Boat Service, and the American, Office for Strategic Services. As with the resistance factions in France, the communication between them on this side of the Channel, was sparse; again due to political reasons and suspicions. George was recruited by the SOE and sent as an agent to organise a resistance Cell in Paris pre-invasion. The SOE may have known what we have only just learned about your family and the French connection. They were meticulous in their search through records; they had to be to ensure the safety and reliance of their agents. It could well have been that George was fluent in French and may well have known Paris very well. In other words, he could fit in with the average Frenchman on the street and not draw attention to himself. What they didn't know, however meticulous they had been, that George was a communist and his trip to France would, unknown to them, have a dual purpose. The SOE had sent him to head up a Cell, with detailed information about the invasion, the location and times of arms drops and a supply of money. This Cell would be instrumental in breaking or slowing down the German lines of communication and transport that would be effective in slowing down their movements after the invasion. Sabotage; blowing up railway lines and telegraph stations that sort of thing. Causing chaos and mayhem and thereby diverting troops away from the invasion landing sites. These sorts of subversive activities were timed and organised to happen around the same time, mainly in the north where the landings would take place, but all over France.'

He paused to take another sip of coffee.

'Blimey Noah,' I said. 'You've been busy.'

'He loves it; don't you Noah,' said Chloe, grinning like a Cheshire cat, as she leaned forward to assemble a few biscuits and cheese together on a side plate.

He nodded and smiled broadly.

'The Second World War isn't really my field, but, yes I am loving this.'

'Let me get this right. Are you saying that George had a different agenda to that of the SOE?' I asked.

He nodded again.

'Yes.'

'I imagine that, that would have been a really dangerous thing to do.'

'I agree. But, you have to realise that at that time, there were double agents and even triple agents. The whole business of spies and infiltrators was incredibly risky. Knowing who to trust with your life and the lives of others, was fraught with dangers and risks, and the possibility of betrayal must have constantly been in their minds.'

'Are you saying that George was a double agent?' asked Chloe.

'It's a little more complicated than that. But...'

'It was to do with politics wasn't it. What was going to happen next in France after the war,' I offered.

He nodded his head.

'Well...a little Alice. It was about revenge. Not vengeance against the Germans, which is in a way what the SOE were sending him for. No. It was about a Frenchman.'

I was a little taken aback.

'A Frenchman?'

'Wow!' said Chloe. 'That's the stuff of films.'

104

He smiled.

'Well, a lot of films were based on such stories. Every man and woman that fought with the resistance were incredibly brave; there's no doubt about that. Many didn't survive. What George did however, was something extraordinarily courageous. After parachuting in and making contact with the French Resistance Cell he had been asked to work with; seemingly, he clandestinely contacted a member of the communist resistance. Doing that could have placed suspicion on him by the very people he was there to help. As I've said, there was a great deal of paranoia at that time. If they found out, it's possible that they could have eliminated him.'

'I can understand that,' I said.

'Me too,' agreed Chloe. 'As you said Noah, the risk of treachery must have kept them very much on edge. They couldn't afford second chances I guess.'

'No. A second chance could mean the difference between life or death; you and your family could be placed in peril. I suppose a lot of innocent people died that way.'

As all this was being discussed, I couldn't help thinking about the man in the gardens. Could what Noah be telling us have some bearing on that? I, more than Noah or Chloe, had another reason for

105

discovering our ancestors' movements and journeys, other than for family history.

Noah continued, 'although I don't have specific details, the next thing that happened was that George was arrested by the Gestapo. I...' he hesitated momentarily, 'I think he purposely got himself arrested.'

'*What!*' I said in disbelief. 'Why would he do that?'

'As I said, I can't be a hundred percent sure, but looking at the arrest papers and records, with which the Germans were notoriously scrupulous about, there was no informer named and the reason for arrest was that he swore at a German soldier. Now, I thought a great deal about the circumstances before his arrest. The fact that he had agent training in Scotland, the fact that, he had met with the French Cell and given them the information they needed and after that, he'd contacted a member of the Communist resistance. It was as if he had completed the mission and the brief of the SOE, and then gave himself up; as improbable as it sounds. If I am right, then you have to ask yourself why? Why take the risk of being exposed, and put your life at risk? Why create a circumstance in which you know it will mean that you will be arrested?'

I thought for a moment.

'Perhaps the communist contact he met with, betrayed him?'

'I did think about that. But, he himself was communist; it was because of that very reason, that he had another agenda when he was sent out to France.'

'Could it have been someone in the French Cell?' Asked Chloe.

'It would appear that he knew where and when to be arrested and where he would be put whilst being questioned. He knew that a French citizen wouldn't be isolated and tortured simply for swearing. I think he knew exactly where he was going and I think I know why he took that risk. And it was a *huge* risk as the situation in Paris at that time, was fluid. Everything was unpredictable. Although not saying so publically, the Germans knew their time was up; that they were witnessing the beginning of the end of the war. So to take the chance in believing precisely, where you would be taken, was, as I said, precarious. The local Police station had, and was at that time, being used for local domestic crime. Suspects and perpetrators were housed in large holding cells. He needed to contact someone whom he knew was being held there; a man who had been caught stealing. George knew that the man, a petty thief, unknowingly had information regarding the identity of a double agent. Information that could lead him to the name of the double agent that had cost the lives of seven of his communist friends in France.'

He paused.

'Did he find out Noah?' I asked.

He shook his head.

'No. I don't think he ever found out. The man he hoped to get the name of the informant from, was moved to another prison before he got the chance to speak with him.'

'How do you know all this Noah?' asked Chloe. 'I mean…'

'I looked at German records, French prison records and reports. I also discovered, by chance really, a biography written by the son of a member of the communist resistance who was based in the same area or Arrondissement of Paris, as George. The author mentioned George. But he never found out who the double agent was.'

'Is the author still alive Noah?'

Both Noah and Chloe looked at me questioningly.

'Erm. I expect so…I don't know? Why?'

'What's the author's name?'

'Benoît Lavigne, pronounced La-veen-ye.'

'What is the book title?'

'Under a Leaden Sky.'

'Why Alice?' asked Chloe.

'Do you have the book Noah?'

'No. It was in the Reference section of the University library.'

I was just about to tell them what had happened in Paris when…

'You may think that, *that* was interesting, 'continued Noah looking directly at me. 'But what I discovered after sitting up most of the last two nights and the ensuing days, chasing up loose ends and verifying what I thought I had found, is…well, is on another level.'

Is this more information about George?' asked Chloe.

Noah shook his head.

'No. This is about his son, your grandfather, Thomas, born in nineteen-thirty seven Shropshire. He's a *lot* more interesting,' he said with a satisfying smile. 'It took some working out I can tell you, which involved frustration and a little swearing to myself; but I think I cracked it.'

I looked at Chloe.

'I don't know much about grandpa Thomas. Do you Chloe?'

She shrugged her shoulders and shook her head.

'No. Not really. I remember going to Shropshire a couple of times when we were kids to see them. But as far as I can remember, I can't recall him ever coming up here to visit us.' Her brow became a little

109

furrowed. 'It's odd really; odd that I've never asked about our Shropshire family.' She looked at me.

'Same with me. I guess it's just that dad never talked about his father. He did a little maybe, but, yeah. I don't know anything about him or grandma. Do you remember seeing grandma when we went to Shropshire?'

A look of puzzlement set across her face. She shook her head.

'Well,' continued Noah. 'Maybe I can fill in a few blank pages for you. I'll set the scene. It's the nineteen sixties. World War Two had ended over fifteen years previously. However, peace was still an uncertainty. It was the time of the Cold War. After the war with Germany and its allies, Communism had gained in strength. It took a foothold in countries such as: Russia, Albania, Bulgaria, China, Czechoslovakia, the former Yugoslavia, Poland, Hungry, Romania, Cuba, North Vietnam, North Korea and after the war when Germany was divided between Russia and the West: it became Communist East Germany, and West Germany, controlled mainly by America and Britain. Those countries believed that the communist ideology, was the way forward. There was mistrust and suspicions on both sides of the divide. It was the same ideology that, as I said earlier, was shared by George and subsequently, adopted by your grandfather, Thomas.'

'My grandpa was a communist?' Questioned Alice. He nodded.

'He was indeed.'

I looked penetratingly at Noah.

'Was he an *active* member of the Communist party?' He stared expressionlessly at me. I continued, 'how do you know for sure?'

He let out a sigh.

'In the documents and papers you gave me; I came across a letter. It wasn't addressed and it had no recipient's name on it. There were three words in it which caught my attention. Black bag assignment.'

Both Chloe and I were clueless. I shrugged my shoulders.

'What does that mean?'

'Well. A Black Bag job is an undercover covert operation to hide surveillance equipment in a building, home, office, to listen in to conversations, or copy files etcetera. These types of operations were named and carried out by the KGB communists during the Cold war.'

The room fell silent momentarily.

'I'm sure our government did the same sort of things, you know, clandestine operations and subversive activities.'

'Indeed we did. Counter intelligence MI5 would have reciprocated. You have to understand that at that time the leaders on all sides were suspicious and I would add, paranoid. Every movement and around every corner they saw ghosts in the machine, and the American CIA agents, or spooks, were just as obsessed and fanatical. Dirty tricks, such as disinformation, subversion, data harvesting, lying, and the use of honey traps.' He looked at us both, 'do you know the term honey trap or honey pot?'

Chloe spoke up.

'Isn't it where spies, usually female, were used to create a sexual or romantic relationship with an agent from the other side, in order to compromise the victim. These liaisons were filmed or photographed, then the photographic evidence, was used to threaten and bribe them to reveal inside information.'

'Couldn't have put it better myself,' said Noah.

Chloe smiled.

'Well…no, you couldn't,' she said with a rascally grin.

Noah continued,' as I said there was so much paranoia, mistrust and confusion at that time, that there were a lot of mistakes and grave errors of judgment; even within their own departments.'

'Did you discover anything else Noah?' I asked.

He shook his head.

'No. Oh, except that the notepaper that the letter was written on, had a French watermark. Nothing unusual there really. Quality writing paper from Europe was beginning to be in vogue at that time.'

I wasn't convinced about the coincidences of what had happened in the park in Paris, the French connection of name changes and constantly shifting addresses and the writing paper. There was something more to it…there was a thread.

I thought it was the right time to reveal to them the story of my trip to Paris and what the man had said to me in the *Jardin des Plantes*…

After I had gone over the events of that day in Paris, they both sat in silence, looking quite perplexed…

'This journey into your past, the family history research for your book, is about what happened in Paris then Alice,' said Noah. 'Jesus. What a thing.' He had a slight look of apprehension about him. I'm guessing that he hadn't seen what I had just told him coming; but then again, who would have?

I nodded.

'It is now about Paris. As you say, it started off innocently enough, that much is true. It was only when you discovered a French connection that it rolled me back to the gardens and what he had said.'

'That must have been a real shock. When I found out about your French ancestry,' said Noah.

I laughed.

'And some.'

'Why didn't you say something Alice?' said Chloe.

'I thought he was just a nutter who had overheard my name and followed me. I just dismissed it. But now…well.' I smiled and let out a sigh.

'What now?' asked Chloe.

I looked at Chloe and then to Noah.

'I hope I'm wrong, but I think I know,' he said, nodding his head slowly.

'What do you mean?' asked Chloe with a quizzical expression.

'I have to go back to Paris.'

'You have *got* to be kidding,' said Chloe.

'Paris is where the answers are. I'm sure, no, I know there is more to this story.'

'*No*! Definitely no,' said Chloe, moving her head from side to side.

'Look I'm a fictional author right, and I'm in the middle of an actual storyline with plots and subplots all over the map.' I looked apologetically at her, 'I have to Chloe.'

Chloe looked at Noah pleadingly.

'Noah?'

He looked at her, then to me and back to Chloe.

'Well thanks for your support Noah,' she said despondently.

'It might be a bit risky Alice,' said Noah. 'You know…on your own. You don't know who to trust.'

'She won't be on her own,' said Chloe. 'I'll be with her.'

I shook my head.

'I'm not being ungrateful, but you can't go Chloe. You have your medical studies. You can't just walk away from that. I want to do this on my own. It started out that way.'

She looked at me and knew me well enough to understand that when I make my mind up, that's pretty much it. Chloe is not like me at all in that respect. She is always willing to compromise and come to an agreement. Chloe and I are very close, but sometimes, we are so very different.

Momentarily, we sat in a reflective silence…

Chloe broke the quietude.

'If you do go, how will you find the man in the park? I presume that's part of your mission?' she said, with a half-cocked smile in recognition of a mind made up.

I smiled at her "compromise and agreement". I looked at Noah. He knew instinctively.

I continued, 'I won't need to.'

115

Chloe looked confused.

'What?'

'He'll find me.'

Chloe shook her head briskly.

'I don't like this Alice. I don't like it at all. Mum and dad would never agree with you going back if they knew.'

'They mustn't know Chloe. Promise me.'

'That's unfair Alice. We never keep anything back from mum and dad.'

Fleetingly, I sat silently…

'I know. But I have to do this.'

She looked at me with her big puppy dog eyes…and she knew.

I had quite a lot of things organised for the following few months and decided that April the following year was the best time to go. And who wouldn't want to be in Paris in the springtime…

CHAPTER TWELVE

Friday 14th April 2023
10:15
Manchester Airport Departure lounge

My flight was delayed, and I arrived at my hotel in Paris, the same hotel as my last stay, rather a lot later than I would have liked.

It had just turned 8pm and as I had not eaten very much prior to boarding, I had decided to get a bite to eat. I left my hotel and walked across the Rue du Petit Pont towards Café le Petit Pont. As I walked over to the outside tables and chairs, the same waiter that I had met previously, was stood by the stand that holds the café menu. He smiled and looked at me.

'Ahh. Bonjour Mademoiselle. You are back with us.'
I was slightly taken-aback. I gave him a broad smile.

'Paris in spring…who would want to be anywhere else.'

He returned an all-encompassing genuine smile.

He pointed to a corner inside the café.

'You sat over there last time I believe.'

I shook my head in disbelief and smiled once more.

'Mon Dieu. That was months ago.'

He nodded, smiled and shrugged his shoulders.

'I will not insult you by saying that I never forget a pretty face.'

I laughed.

'Please do.'

He laughed and continued, 'you are joining us for for food, or a drink maybe?'

I let out a sigh.

'Food. My flight was delayed. I should have been here hours ago. I'm famished.'

He tipped his head to one side appeasingly.

'Still, you are here now. Maybe this time a table alfresco?'

I nodded spiritedly.

'Oh yes please.'

He unfurled his arm and I followed the direction of his hand, 'how about here.'

I nodded.

'Here, is just right.'

He smiled.

118

At the table, he pulled out a chair and I sat down. He placed the menu in front of me.

'Please take your time Mademoiselle.'

I smiled.

'Alice.'

He gave me a convivial smile.

'Well, it is no wonder you are drawn to France; you have a French name.'

Momentarily, a cold chill ran down my spine. What with all the French connection information that Noah gave me and the man in the park and the very reason for me being back in France...well, it just shocked me a little. I must have shown it in my expression.

The waiter looked a little concerned.

'You are alright mademoiselle?'

I managed to relax and offered him a reassuring smile.

'Yes thank you. It's just been a long day. And please. Alice.'

He smiled.

'And if it is not too presumptuous, I am Pascal.'

I nodded and smiled.

'Well...there we are then.'

He returned the smile.

'I'll leave you to choose your food.'

He turned and walked over to another of the patron's table.

I ordered my food and as I waited, I thought about the situation, and to be quite honest, with all my bravado and confidence; I was feeling a little apprehensive. I looked around me at the others in the café: were any of them part of what I was here for? Do they know? I looked across, and up and down the rue de la Bûcherie. Everyone suddenly became a shady suspect…my mind was in freefall and I had to snap out of it. I looked towards Shakespeare and Company and listened to the relaxed laughter and conversations, which began to settle me and ease my mind. It was ridiculous supposing everyone around me was in some kind of plot. It was my writer's mind and imagination I guess, running away with itself. And actually, even with the weirdness of it all, why was I thinking that I could be at risk. Nothing that the man in the park had said made me feel that I was in any danger. Yes, it was disconcerting, but nothing threatening or putting me in jeopardy. And anyway, I don't know what I was getting so giddy goat about; it had been my decision to return and pursue it. I now became more laid-back and began to enjoy being back in this beautiful and scenic city, and retune my mind to allow me to see how it pans out. Sans souci, as the French say; "without worry".

After a delightful meal, I felt a little tired and I decided to go back to hotel and hit the sack. Tomorrow, I would revisit *Jardin des Plantes* ...

CHAPTER THIRTEEN

Saturday 15th April 2023
11:47
Jardin des Plantes

After breakfast at the hotel and a very pleasant walk retracing my previous amble along the river Seine, I arrived at *Jardin des Plantes.* It was busier than the last time I visited, but the gardens are spacious enough to absorb a great number of visitors without if feeling confining or claustrophobic. I sought out the bench I had previously sat on. It was vacant. I sat down and waited. The feeling I had was of motivated anticipation; controlled, but an eager expectancy…

Minutes turned to hours. I couldn't wait any longer, I was getting bored, hungry and with all this waiting, a little anxiety was beginning to creep in. The situation was making me feel uneasy and I didn't have to put myself through that. I stood and turned to walk back towards the river.

A voice came from behind.

'Hello Alice.' Without seeing him; I knew it was he.

Calmly, I sat down on the bench and he sat at the other end to me; once again allowing us to communicate but leaving a respectful space between us.

I looked at him. He gave me a reassuring smile. I have a feel for picking up on people's auras and personalities; I don't know whether it's genetic or an acquired skill of the author, to carefully observe people, their habits, traits and their surroundings. There didn't seem to be anything sinister about this man. Even though he, or more precisely, his words had haunted me and driven me back to Paris, his kind eyes, gave out a reassuring warmth and his body language was easy, relaxed and understated.

'You are back in our beautiful city once more Alice,' he said offering another comforting smile.

I looked at him unemotionally.

'You know my name, I think it would be courteous of you, to tell me yours.'

He nodded and smiled.

'My name is Benoît. Benoît Lavigne.'

I could feel every hair on the back of my neck rise up, added to the cold chill running down my spine.

I continued, 'Under a leaden sky…your book.'

123

He sat back into the bench; he was clearly surprised; I would say, a little shocked. He nodded his head slowly and knowledgably, and gave me a broad smile.

'Bravo Alice.'

I don't know why, but I returned the smile.

'Bravo indeed.'

I paused momentarily before saying to him, '"You are not who you think yourself to be". Interesting thing to say to a total stranger. A stranger who was just enjoying the day and her time in Paris…a rather special time, I should add, that could have had the edge taken of it by such a weird and irritating statement.'

He smiled and nodded.

'Hmm. Yes. I see your point.'

He was almost blasé in his response. I became a little annoyed.

'Right now, at this very moment, I feel like buying a large baguette and hitting you over the head with it.'

He shrugged his shoulders nonchalantly.

'It would be a shame to waste food, when so many in this World are going without.'

I was gobsmacked. I held up my hands questioningly.

'You want me to explain Alice?'

'Do I even need to answer that?'

124

'I will come to my "irritating statement" a little later. Firstly, as you know the title of my book, you must also be aware of its context. Am I correct?'
'I haven't read it. But, a friend has given a little of the background.'
He raised his eyebrows questioningly.
'You have *not* read it?'
'Correct.'

I went over what all that Noah had uncovered about my great grandfather George and his activities as a SOE agent and communist, and how he got himself arrested in order to get information or uncover the truth about the betrayal of his fellow communists from a prisoner in the same jail; but had failed...

After a few moments in silence, he spoke, 'your friend, Noah, has done some surprising research, however, all is not how it seems. It is altered slightly.'
'How is it different?'
'George was a SOE agent, he did get himself arrested, but he wasn't a communist.'
I was puzzled.
'He wasn't?'
He shook his head.

'No. He wasn't. When it came to the communists, he was a double agent. He fabricated his beliefs and ideology, in order to penetrate the French communist resistance. It is complicated to explain, but you have to understand that there was so much uncertainty, mistrust, betrayals and deceit in France at that time. The resistance movements distrusted each other. On the sixteenth and seventeenth of July 1942 in an act known as the Vel' d'Hiv, the Roundup of Jews in Paris took place. This included more than 4,000 children. Many French born Jews fled to support the various résistance movements and cells that were beginning to organise themselves to begin to plan subversive operations. At this time, the résistance movement was in its infancy; of which there were several factions. Later on in time, there was a seemingly disproportionate capture of French Jewish resistance fighters. Simply put, they were being betrayed. Was it the French Gaullists, the Maquis, or was it the communists? There was too much coincidence for it to be ordinary citizens. Although it did sometimes occur where personal grudges, dislikes, or something as simple as a neighbour dispute, would lead to a betrayal and arrest. Your great grandfather George's reason for coming to France during the war, was to find out who was betraying the French Jewish résistance fighters. The SOE believed it to be the communists. The man he wanted to speak to in the jail, was a French Jew, not a communist…he was my father.'

I sat mesmerised by what he had said, that turned what Noah had told me on its head. I sat silently momentarily trying to take in and make some sense of it all. How had Noah got it so wrong? I smiled to myself. I couldn't wait to get back and tell him that!

'So, do you know if my grandfather Thomas, was a communist during the Cold war? It's all a little fuzzy. Noah had evidence that supports that he was.'

He looked to the floor and then back to me.

'With all respects; Noah had evidence to support the story of George being a communist; and he wasn't.' He let out a sigh. 'Counter espionage is about that very thing: disinformation, deception half-truths; creating illusions…smoke and mirrors.'

I shook my head.

'*Phew!*'

My mind was in a bit of a whirl to be honest. I don't know what I was expecting by coming back to Paris; but everything so far, had been extraordinary, and unexpected. There was a part of me that wanted the answer to his initial "irritating statement" and my connection to all of what he had told me so far…right now. However, and as crazy as it might seem, the writer in me wanted the story to unravel and slowly reveal itself, as it would in a novel. I don't know; I must be wired differently or something. What was I even doing sat on a bench, listening to a total interloper, telling me about *my* family. Did I believe him? I really didn't know at that moment. I nodded and smiled.

He sat and looked at me in silence momentarily allowing me a moment or two in which to gather my thoughts…

'Your family history Alice is as complex as it is interesting.'

'Yes, I'm beginning to see that,' I said rather impishly.

'We have all come from somewhere in time and each of us have our own stories. Sometimes however, if we can unravel them, some are a little more interesting than others.'

I looked at him.

'There's more isn't there.' It was rhetorical.

He nodded.

'Yes Alice. There is more.'

'Is it about Thomas and the Cold war?'

He sat thoughtfully momentarily.

'There is more about Thomas. But…'

'But?'

'I would like to take you back to the beginning of this. To explain to you where you have come from, and why, and how, I know about you.'

I looked thoughtfully, but intently at him.

'Would you like to hear that story Alice?'

I nodded meaningfully.

'Are you kidding me. Yes, Benoît. I would.'

He smiled then let out a deep and expressive sigh.

'OK. I have written a summary for you in a letter, which I have in my pocket, it also contains some other information; in which there is a significant detail that I think you will find to be of great interest. I've written it down for you, as what I am about to tell you, you might find complicated and confusing. I have to take you back to the year 1209, Béziers in the Occitanie region of France. At this time the Catholic Church was all-powerful. Any threat to undermine it was dealt with in the most brutal and ruthless way.

In Béziers at this time, there were many religious denominations that all lived peacefully together, including French Jews and Cathars. The Jews held many businesses and were well known in that part of the country as excellent traders and bankers. They became so influential that the church and the King, Philip II, began to feel uneasy about the power that they had. It set about the task of removing that threat. Today you might call it ethnic

129

cleansing. However, the Jews were so prominent and important to the functioning of society at that time, that any move to eradicate them could have had serious consequences on the church. There were many powerful Counts who supported and worked with the Jews. It was a very complex situation, one in which the church had to take great care. They needed an excuse, and many believe that they created a credible deception. Pope Innocent III sent one of his most trusted ecclesiastic scholar's and Cistercian Monk, Pierre de Castelnau to meet with Raymond VI, Count of Toulouse who was a supporter of the Jews and Cathars. He was sent with the soul purpose to discuss the place of the Cathars in church and state. However, on his return, he was murdered. It was alleged by the church that Pierre de Castelnau was assassinated on the instruction of Raymond. But, this would not have made any sense. *Cui bono.*' He looked at me.

'Yes. I know what that means.'

'Who stands to gain or benefit from such an act?

 As Raymond had nothing to gain from the monk's death, it must be concluded that instruction for the slaying must have come from the church. *They* were to benefit.'

'How?'

'After, what was claimed by the church in propaganda through word of mouth and writing, as

130

a heinous and brutal crime against the church, committed by a powerful Count, but on behalf of the Cathars, offered the church and the King an opportunity to rid themselves of the Jews. The King sent a Simon de Montfort who was known for his opposition and hostility towards the Cathars, to lay siege in Béziers. The town was besieged. The Catholics were offered the freedom to leave unharmed. But many refused and took the decision to stay along side their Cathar and Jewish friends. What followed was the slaughter of, it is estimated, seven thousand men, women and children; some contemporary academics say that it was possibly up to as many as twenty thousand.' He paused and looked at me. The look of disbelief on my face must have been palpable.

'You see Alice, through that one small deception, the church and the King were able to rid themselves of the Jews and sequestrate and confiscate their money, businesses, lands and properties. The Cathars, were a ruse. They lived simply and piously. Yes, the church did perceive them as a threat to the Catholic orthodoxy, but it was the Jews they were after in Béziers. They held the financial power; the Cathar threat was about belief. But belief in piety does not make you financially wealthy; only spiritually.'

'I've heard of the name Simon de Montfort.'

131

He looked at me and smiled broadly.

'Hmm.'

I looked questioningly at him.

'Simon de Montfort went on to commit more atrocities in Carcassonne and then later as Earl of Leicester, he once again targeted the Jews. He expelled them from the City and cancelled all debts owed to them. Tragically, the slaughter continued in London, Worcester and Derby. On banishing them, from Leicester, he said, "In my time or in the time of any of my heirs to the end of the World" to justify it he further said, "for the good of my soul, and for the souls of my ancestors and successors".'

Once again he paused and looked at me...

'In Béziers at that time, lived a man, his wife and son. They were Robert de Merclesden, his wife Alice,' he looked at me and smiled, then continued, 'and their son, Richard. At the time of the siege, Robert and his son Richard were in Toulouse on business. On their return Robert discovered that his wife, Alice had been burned alive with so many others. He was taken with such a rage that it had a direct impact and consequences on events that were to follow. On the 4th August 1265 at the battle of Evesham, England, Simon de Montfort was killed. Instruction was given to dismember his body. Robert's son, Richard de Merclesden was one of the Knights. He castrated Simon and placed the testicles into Simon's mouth. This act was to avenge the brutal murder of his mother, Alice.'

'*Bloody hell*!'

'It was a bloody time Alice; the Middle ages. This act of dismembering was witnessed by one of Simon's knights. He managed to flee the battle site and survive. He was an exception. No quarter was given and nearly everyone else was hunted down and pitilessly killed. It was a rout…a massacre.'

'Forgive me for asking, but I'm a little puzzled as to where my ancestry fits in with all this.'

He gave me a broad smile and continued, 'the Knight who had witnessed the final act of atrocity on Simon, and believe me, the whole battle was a day of inhumane atrocities, vowed that he would avenge Simon's death. Two years had passed by when he finally tracked down Richard de Merclesden. He found him by the river Tay in Scotland watering his horse. He took him by surprise and held his head under water until he drowned.'

'Can I just ask. Are there any happy moments ahead in this conversation? Only, so far, it's not been very jolly…interesting and informative, but a little, you know, depressing.'

Once again the broad smile returned.

'So, Richard's drowning was witnessed by *his* son, Thomas aged 11. As he released Richard's body into

133

the river, he turned and saw the young boy hiding in the reeds. What happened next you might think a little strange. The boy was now an orphan as his mother had died previously...'

'*Oh please!*'

He laughed.

'He took him back to France with him and through a sort of penance or benevolence, adopted him.'

'Ahh, *at last!*'

'The man who had made him become an orphan, was called, Hugh de Rochambeau. The boy became, Thomas Rochambeau.'

My blood ran cold. Rochambeau! That was the name of my Great Great Grandfather X 2, Louis Rochambeau, born 1857, that Noah had discovered who changed his name to Garner after his wife's maiden name, Yevette Garnier (Gar-nee-yay) when they moved from France to England. I held my hands up.

'Right, hang on a moment...let me think about this.'

All the words were swirling around in my head like confetti in a vortex, and then slowly they dropped into sentences, that I began to decipher.

'So, let me get this right. Am I right in thinking that my ancestors were originally called de Merclesden?'

He smiled and nodded.

'Yes.'

'Then, Rochambeau, and then Garner.'

He smiled.

'Yes. That's exactly right.'

We sat there unspoken for a little time as I processed what I had learned…

'*Wow*! Well, it was worth the price of a budget airline ticket, I can tell you that.'

Then the question that prompted me to return came back to me.

'Are we family Benoît?'

Again, the broad warm smile.

'No.'

I returned the smile.

He passed me an impish smile.

'Are you disappointed Alice? '

'No,' I replied indifferently.

He seemed a little put out.

I gave him a heartfelt smile.

'To be honest Benoît, yes, I am a little. But what's puzzling me is, why and how do you know all this about my family?'

He let out a sigh.

'I stumbled across it to be honest. There *is* a connection between us. My family came from a similar brutal circumstance. A different town, but we received similar treatment from the church, and from that time we have endeavoured to remember

135

what happened and to communicate the truth to all these matters. A Knight, who fought in the battle of Evesham on the side of the King, was one of my ancestors. He played no part in the dismembering of Simon de Montfort. He refused on the grounds of Chivalry. What took place at Evesham and what consequently happened to Simon, was an extremely unchivalrous act. An action, which at the time, was quietly condemned by many of the King's followers. My ancestor and his family paid a dear price for his refusal to take part in Simon's mutilation. Many years after the young boy Thomas was adopted, he turned away from violence and war and was drawn towards learning and education. He became a great scholar. It was during his research that he persuaded his foster father, Hugh de Rochambeau, that although Simon de Montfort was the perpetrator and instrument of the Church and King; he had been deceived and used by them to carry out what they wouldn't do for themselves. They didn't want to be seen to have blood on their hands. After the exposé and truth emerged, especially to Hugh de Rochambeau, they both pledged an oath to right the injustices and atrocities that had been carried out in the name of the King and the church. My ancestor joined with them in their quest. So, a small, but significant connection.'

Once again I had to think for a moment…

'All this still travels from *so* long ago Benoît.'
'Yes. I do have a day job.' He laughed.
'Are you a Cathar Benoît?'
He shook his head.
'No. There are a few that continue the journey from that time. They are called, *Défenseur de la Foi – Defender of the faith or truth.* It's a little Dan Brown I know.' He shrugged his shoulders and smiled.
I laughed.
'More Kate Mosse I'd say.'
'It's similar.'
He nodded and shrugged his shoulders once again.
'They are not religious zealots; they just try to find where the truth is.'
'Are you one of *them*?'
He shook his head.
'When I was a boy, my father told me stories about our family. I have been interested in family history, ever since. Unlike the *Défenseur de la Foi,* for me, it is a passion rather than a way of life.'
'They must have upset a few people along the way.'
With raised eyebrows and a schoolboy grin he replied, 'yes. I suppose they must have done.'
I smiled and nodded.
'Something else that puzzles me.'

Again he raised his eyebrows, this time inquisitively.

'How could you possibly know when I would arrive here? The first time I came, we had never met, yet you knew I would be arriving; where and when. That day here in the gardens is obviously no coincidence? And now, today?'

He settled back into the bench, looked at me and sat in silence momentarily…

'I cannot tell you that Alice.'

'You can't tell me?' I was slightly taken aback. 'Well that's just great! Yeah. Thanks for that.'

'I and a few friends do belong to a…erm, how can I say, a secret organisation and it is better that you don't know.'

'Well that's convenient.'

He looked puzzled.

'How do you mean?'

'Well, you seem to know an awful lot about my family and me. On the one hand, you appear to be caring and thoughtful, and yet, behind the masque there is another man.' I looked down at the floor. Weirdly, my words "behind the masque" is exactly what my novel - if ever it got past Chapter One - was going to be called. 'Can you tell me what it is you do?'

He looked thoughtfully for a moment.

'We solve puzzles…tie up loose ends.'

138

I knew my line of questioning was not going to go anywhere anytime soon. I changed tack.

'I'm a novelist…but of course you know that already, So, as a novelist, I'm always looking for inspiration. Could you give me any ideas for a good plot?'

He smiled broadly and tipped his head to his left shoulder.

'Hmm. I would say that you don't have to look too far into the distant past. There would be a good story in your own family Alice.'

I narrowed my eyes reflectively. I was trying to read his thoughts. For some reason, I had the feeling that he wasn't talking about the medieval "stuff". But, what happened in World War Two or the events that took place during the nineteen-sixties.

'Communists?'

He looked expressionlessly at me.

'Tread carefully Alice. The ground beneath your feet is not always as secure and trustworthy, as you believe it to be.'

That little piece of information set the creative part of my brain whirling. At, the same time, it also sent sent a chill down my spine. There was a certainty in his voice, and I knew that he was not going to give any more away.

Acquiescently, I nodded.

'OK Benoît.'

He smiled warmly.

'I do have a little more to tell you Alice, but I have to be somewhere else…' he looked at his watch, 'Right now actually.'

'*More* Benoît?' I said with a playful grin.

He gave me a big smile.

'When are you flying back home?'

I raised my eyebrows curiously.

'You mean you don't know?' I said with another impish smile. 'You seem to know everything else about me.' He grimaced.

'Tomorrow night.'

He nodded thoughtfully and smiled.

'I know you might want some time to yourself, but could we meet for dinner. As I said, I do have something else to tell you. But I really must go now.'

'Café le petit pont?'

'Perfect. Shall we say…seven-thirty?'

'That fits for me.'

He and I both stood. We looked at each other, the uncertainty replaced by a common bond; we hugged each other.

'Thank you so much Benoît…I think?'

He laughed, turned, and without looking back, waved and walked towards the garden exit. I sat down once again on the bench…this time quite alone with my feelings and my thoughts. He had left the garden when I realised something.

'*The letter*!' I said rather too loudly, making a female passer-by's eyes widen perceptibly. The letter that he said was a summary of what he had revealed to me, plus, I think he had said that it also contained some other important information.

'Bugger,' I muttered under my breath. I was certain though that he would remember and bring it along with him to the Café le petit pont.

I took myself for a stroll along the river. The sun was shining and the local artisans were selling their wares along the river embankment wall. This unwavering and unchanging pace of life: the river flowing gently under historical bridges, the cheery and I guess, mischievous and occasionally rude remarks of the traders to each other, the tourists ever smiling and constantly taking photos; the café culture and the Parisians far too busy to engage in conversation or make eye contact with vacationers. All this, untainted and unaffected by the drama that was unfurling in my life.

It had been quite a day. As a writer, I was enthralled by the revelations. But because of my literary mind, I could envisage all kinds of scenarios. I sat down on a bench by the river as the tourist Batobus sailed by me. I quite envied them;

they were of clear minds thinking only of enjoyment and capturing the moment as it flies: sharing a joke, laughing, telling stories and playful lovers holding each other tenderly, as the romantic city of Paris glided by.

For me, the happy innocent event of my visit to Shakespeare and Company and of being just that, a tourist, was a distant reverie. My mind was in a spin. I really didn't understand what was happening to me; and for me, always being focussed and confident, it was a little unsettling. Hopefully, I thought to myself, tonight might bring with it some kind of closure…

CHAPTER FOURTEEN

Saturday 15th April 2023
19:23
Café le petit pont,
paris

I managed to find a vacant table outside.

A voice came from behind me.

'Hello again.'

I turned to see the smiling and welcoming face of Pascal the waiter.

'Good evening Pascal. How are you?'

He seemed a little bemused, his smile quickly returning.

'Well. I am *very* good thank you. And *how* are you this evening?'

I nodded and smiled.

'I am also very well.'

'That is good.'

'Are you just having a drink, or are you dining with us?'

'Dining.'

'OK. I'll get the menu for you, and the specials are on the board,' he pointed, 'just there.'

He was just about to clear away the other set cutlery from the table.

'Thank you Pascal. I'm waiting for a friend to join me.'

He raised his eyebrows and smiled.

'Of course.' He replaced the cutlery for two.

'I'll fetch two menus.'

I returned a warm smile.

'Thank you.'

He turned and walked away.

He had been away from the table for a couple of minutes, when, I heard an audible muffled thud followed by a woman screaming. Others walking by on the pavement on the road nearby pointed; one young girl held her hand to her mouth as in disbelief. It was difficult to see from where I was sitting. But from what I could make out from the direction that people were rushing in, whatever had happened, had occurred on or near to the Pont Notre-Dame.

Within minutes, emergency vehicles were in attendance and the road cordoned off. I looked at my phone...it was 19:52. I couldn't believe how quickly the time had passed. I was just wondering where Pascal was when a voice from behind interrupted my thoughts. This time there was urgency about it...

'Mademoiselle.'

I turned.

'Yes Pascal?' he seemed quite distressed.

'You must come with me please.'

I narrowed my eyes in bewilderment.

'I'm sorry Pascal. What do you mean?'

He bent over to me and whispered in a serious tone.

'You must come with me Alice. Please. It is important that you do this now.'

I don't know why I didn't question him. I stood and followed him into the kitchen. He opened the back door and pointed to a car that was parked there. He closed the door behind us. He walked over to the passenger door and opened it for me.

'Please Alice.'

I was so apprehensive, and beginning to feel a little panicky.

'No. I'm sorry Pascal. I can't get in there. You must understand that?'

'You must Alice. It is not safe for you to stay here.'

146

'What are you *talking* about? Not safe? *Why* is it not safe?'

'There has been an accident. A serious accident.'

'Yes I thought I heard something. But…'

'You are waiting for Benoît are you not?'

I was completely caught off guard.

'Yes. How did you *know* that?'

The accident. It was Benoît. He…' A look of distress set over his face, and I could see that there were tears welling. I was so confused. How did he *possibly* know that *I* knew Benoît?

'What *is it* Pascal? What's happened?'

'A man has been hit by a car. It is Benoît.'

'Benoît?' I was stunned.

Struggling to hold his tears back, he continued, 'Benoît, is my father. He…he is dead Alice.'

My mind instantly fell into a spiral.

'Benoît. Your father?' I whispered in utter bewilderment.

'Yes. You must come with me. Please it is not safe for you here.'

'But I don't *understand* Pascal. Why do *I* have to *go* with you?' I shook my head. 'You should be with your father?'

He looked at me pleadingly.

'I understand Alice. I *will* explain. But we must go now. It is urgent we leave here. Please. You have to trust me.'

147

I looked at him. His body language and his mournful yet determined expression, told me that I should go with him. Without further hesitation, I got into the car and closed the door. He got in and in silence we set off to god knows where and to god knows what?

I went over the last hour or so, and questioned myself as to why *I* had to flee? As sad and shocking as it was; his father had died tragically in an accident. Why and how, has that misfortune seemingly, put *me* in jeopardy?

After ten minutes or so driving in total silence, he pulled up into a layby by the river. Remaining silent, his head now bowed. I didn't know what to do, or say. I did what comes naturally; I reached out to a fellow human being who was distraught and clearly in pain. I placed my arm around his shoulder and comforted him.

We sat there for a further few minutes before he lifted his head and stared out of the windscreen deep in thought. Then he turned his head and asked, 'When is your flight home Alice?'
The last person to ask me that, was his father.
'Tomorrow night.'
Once again he sat staring out of the windscreen before turning once more to me.

148

'There are things that we have to talk about Alice, and I will explain as much as I know, to you. But first, you must contact your airline to see if you can change your flight to tonight.'

'*Tonight?*'

'Yes Alice. Tonight.'

'There might not *be* a later flight. And anyway, I can't fly back tonight.'

'You will not be flying back.'

'I don't understand? You want me to change my flight to one that I won't be going on?

'There is a lot to do and arrange, and very little time. You must trust me Alice. Please. I know that this is difficult and inexplicable for you to understand.'

There was such an earnest honesty in his voice, and considering what devastation had just happened in his life; a calmness.

I took out my phone and checked for flights leaving later tonight.

'There is a flight at 23:20.'

'Are there any available seats?'

I put in the details.

'Yes.'

'OK. Can you change your flight booking?'

'Erm…yes, I think so.'

'Do it please.'

149

I typed in all the details. It wouldn't allow me to alter it.

'I can't do it. It's telling me to contact them.'

'OK.'

I typed in the number and it rang…and rang…and rang. Then the options: my head was pounding so much it hurt.

'Ah yes hello. I wonder if you can help me. I'll give you my flight details.' I read them out and she found my booking. 'I have to leave urgently tonight. Is it possible to change my booking?'

She said it was possible for a small charge. I gave her my card details and it was done.

'Thank you.'

I looked at him.

'What now Pascal?'

'I'll drive you close to your hotel. Tell them that you will be checking out early; that something has come up at home and you have to leave urgently and that you have changed your flight. Pack your case and then meet me where I drop you. It is where the taxies wait. I'm not allowed to park there, but I can pick you up.'

'Then what? And why if I'm not going home, have I changed my flight to tonight?' It must be the writer in me, because as I asked him the questions…it suddenly occurred to me as to the why?

150

I checked out of the hotel and wheeled my suitcase to the taxi rank.

'Do you require a taxi mademoiselle?' came a voice from the lowered side window of a taxi?

Just then Pascal pulled up. I wheeled my case over to the car, put my case inside the boot, closed it and got in the passenger side, much to the consternation of the taxi driver. Pascal drove off. To where, I knew not, into what kind of situation, I also knew not. But I had the feeling that my life, would never be the same again...

CHAPTER FIFTEEN

We had been on the road for about 3 hours with very few words passing between us, when we arrived at a small town. He drove a little further on before pulling into a 24-hour supermarket on the outskirts of the town. I was already confused; but why are we now in a supermarket car park?

'I have just remembered Alice. You came to the café for a meal...that you didn't get. You must be hungry. We can get something here if you like. It is probably the only place that will open at this time.'

I nodded.

'I am hungry to be honest Pascal.'

He parked up under the boughs of a large plane tree. I was just about to get out of the car...

'I think you should wait here Alice. Tell me what you would like and I'll get it for you.'

'Why? I mean...I don't understand? I don't know what I want without...Why can't I come with you?'

He let out a sigh.

'It is a difficult time for us both. I will explain a little more when we arrive at our destination.'

He could see that I clearly couldn't grasp why I couldn't go into the supermarket.

He looked at me appeasingly.

'I don't think we should be seen together on CCTV.'

That little snippet of information rooted me firmly to the seat I can tell you. I think along with the death of Benoît, fleeing from the café, cancelling my flight home and not getting on it, being driven to god knows where and now being told that I cannot be seen on CCTV; made me feel threatened by a situation; a predicament, in which for once in my life, I had no control, or understanding of.

'I will give you answers. Please believe me Alice.'

He sounded genuine and his eyes looked so trustworthy.

I nodded.

'A cheese salad baguette or similar, a really strong coffee and a cake of your choice, to share.'

He let out a small but meaningful smile.

'OK.'

He got out of the car, closed the door and walked off towards the supermarket. With what had happened and what was unfurling, as I watched him walk away, my fictitious thoughts took over with varying scenarios. Now, you don't have to be a writer to imagine the "what if". We have all seen enough films

153

and TV dramas. What if a car runs *him* down as he crosses the car park? What if somebody comes to the car and drags me from it? I reached over turned his key and put the door locks on. What if he is linked to some sort of clandestine organisation? What if he lied and he isn't Benoît's son? Well, I didn't really like any of those scenarios to be honest; so, more positively, I looked forward to my baguette and cake. This rather more pleasant scenario was replaced by the need for the bathroom!

After about 10 minutes or so I could see Pascal leaving the supermarket and walking back to the car. He opened the door and placed a carrier bag on the back seat. He got into the car and closed the door. He turned, looked at me and smiled warmly.
'All good.'
'What is?'
'I think you will like the cake.'
'To share.'
He smiled again and nodded.
'To share.'
'I think we might have a slight issue Pascal.'
He looked concerned.
'I need the bathroom.'
He raised his eyebrows.
'Ahh. I see.'
He started up his engine.
He cleared his throat affectedly.

'How can I say this. Do you *need* the bathroom, or would a quiet place be…erm. If you need it, you could ask in the supermarket. I'm sure they must have bathroom facilities.' Although it was a good intent, he looked a little nervous at me getting out of the car here.

I smiled.

'Just a pee; somewhere quiet would be nice.'

He drove out through the town and into the countryside. We came to a layby next to a hedgerow.

'Is here OK?'

I nodded.

'Here will be just fine.'

We decided to stay in the layby to eat.

'How far away are we Pascal?'

'It is about another two hours.'

'Can I ask where we are going?'

He smiled.

'Yes of course. Saint-Goustan. I have a good friend who has a home there. He is in America at the moment but I have a key.' He hung his head in a deep reflection. I sensed his pain and loss. I placed my hand on top of his. He began to weep gently.

We sat in silence…

'I am so sorry Pascal. I only met your father twice, but he seemed a very kind and caring human being.'

He managed a small but kind-hearted smile.

'He was a good soul and my dearest friend.'

I gave him a few more moments for reflection...

'I am sorry to ask Pascal, but...'

'I know Alice. It is complicated and we are both a little tired I feel. If I could explain in detail tomorrow after we have had a little rest.'

I nodded.

'OK Pascal. Can I just ask why we are going to Saint-Goustan? Is it important?'

'It is a safe place in which we can gather our thoughts and plan what to do next. It will be come clearer tomorrow I promise. Well, as much as I can tell you from what I know.'

'You don't know *precisely* then?'

He shook his head.

'Not all.'

A small, but significant cloud appeared over my head.

In a little over two hours, we arrived in Saint-Goustan. At first glance it looked to be a very pretty medieval town.

With my suitcase placed in the bedroom and our "goodnights" said, we turned in for the night. With all that had happened, I thought I might find it difficult to nod off; I was out like a light...

CHAPTER SIXTEEN

Sunday 16th April 2023

Saint-Goustan

I awoke and looked at my phone, the time was 09:27. I had showered and freshened up before deciding on what to wear. I knew it was going to be another day of disclosures and I wanted to be dressed ready for it. Well, that's what us girls do isn't it? Priorities and all that…

I opened the door and walked into the kitchen. It was surprisingly a good size. From what I recalled from my arrival in the early hours, albeit a little hazy, the external proportions of the house didn't really lend itself to having a large kitchen and actually, such a big bedroom. Still, what do I know about properties. I still live at home with my parents.

Pascal was sat at the table. He looked up. His face was a little sorrowful and his eyes heavy and ringed with lack of sleep. He managed a smile.

'Good morning Alice.'

'Good morning Pascal.' I was going to ask him how he was, but stopped short, as I could clearly see it in his demeanour, and it might have triggered him. As I have said before, sometimes it's the space between words that has more meaning.

He held up a cafetiere. His eyes became a little brighter.

'Coffee.'

I smiled.

'Strong?'

He grinned.

'Very.'

I smiled again and nodded.

'Yes please.'

As he poured the aroma filled the air and suffused my nostrils; the sensation was simply lovely.

'I raised the cup and took a sip.'

Pascal sat staring at me with an easy smile. He nodded.

'Good?'

'Yes. Very good,' I said offering him a warm-hearted smile.

'Breakfast?'

I shook my head.

'I'm OK for now. Thank you.'

He nodded once more and smiled.

We sat in silence for a few moments…

'So?' I asked.

He nodded

'I have to make a couple of calls…' He gazed reflectively at the floor before looking up at me and continuing. '…regarding my father's arrangements and also trying to establish precisely, what happened.'

'I…I have found it difficult to understand why you left your father and didn't stay with him Pascal?'

159

'I had no choice. Hopefully, I can give you the details after the phone calls, if that's OK Alice? I know it is important to you to know, I understand that, of course I do, and you have been extraordinarily understanding and cooperative; but firstly, I have to make the arrangements and get more information for myself. I hope that's OK?'

'Yes of course it is Pascal. Do what you have to.'

I looked out of the kitchen window down through a narrow alleyway with crook timbered buildings lining the lane.

'It looks so beautiful.'

'It is.'

'I'll go for a walk while you make your calls. It'll give you some space.'

I sensed a little doubt. He rubbed his chin.

'You seem a little hesitant?'

He smiled.

'Yes. I think that would alright Alice.'

His uncertainty, made my mind begin its journey to yet more scenarios.

'If you think I shouldn't…'

'No. It will be OK. Just…take care.'

I nodded. I think I know what he meant; be observant and watchful. But be vigilant of what exactly?

I smiled.

'I will Pascal.'

We exchanged phone numbers, before closing the door behind me, and walking out onto the narrow lane.

The exterior of the old stone houses abutting the lane, were adorned by clematis, ivy, wisteria and other climbing plants. Where any space allowed, pots planted with multifarious brightly coloured plants spilled over the rims painting the scene as Monet may have contemplated.

Within a few minutes I was at the harbour. It was small and very pretty. I walked on a little further and found a bench overlooking the river. For the first time since…well, what seemed to me to be days, which was really just over a day, I had found a little corner of peace. As I sat there, I tried to make sense of all that had happened. With a literary surgical precision, I dissected each moment. The events as a whole, were puzzling, perplexing and confusing. The one thing that I found concerning more than any of the other parts of the total, is why *did* Pascal leave his father at the scene of the accident? What drove him to place a hypothetical threat to my safety, over spending the last few moments with him? I guess, I hoped, he would explain that to me later as he had promised; so I didn't dwell on that point. I did though try to analyse why I might be at risk? Was it a connection to the Cathars, was it related to the medieval Jews and the slaughter which perhaps later resurfaced in the second world war, or perhaps it didn't re-emerge; was it perhaps a continuation of hatred, revenge and oaths made and passed down through generations? Even for my creative mind…it was all a bit of a mess really. Benoît's father had been the man incarcerated by the Germans and George my great grandfather who was in the SOE had tried to make contact with him, why? I do know now that what Noah had told me; might not be entirely correct. I guess even for an academic, things can occasionally get misinterpreted. I slumped back into the bench. Benoît had said to me that the organisation he was affiliated to, "tied up loose ends and solved puzzles". I could sure do with some of that right now…just a little bit of that.

I watched the various types of boats bobbing meditatively on the calm and tranquil water's skin. I thought about my present family. Then, and why it had taken so long I don't know, a thought flew into my mind so vehemently that it delivered a pain to my head. Does my dad know about any of this? I sat bolt upright. 'Oh my god!' I whispered. If I am in danger; are they? My little corner of peace by the tranquil river, had just become an anchorage for paranoia. Then it occurred to me that I should be arriving back in the UK today. I had to phone my sister. But what to say to her? I decided to tell her that I would be spending a little more time being a tourist. Simple as that...

After a brief easy conversation with her, I had convinced her that I found Paris to be too irresistible - which it is, to leave early.

I had spotted a lovely little café and had just stood up to get myself a coffee, when my phone rang out. It was Pascal.

'Hello Pascal.'

'Hello Alice. Is everything OK?'

'Yes. I'm just by the harbour.'

There was a moment's pause...

'I'll come and meet you there.'

'OK. I've just seen a nice little café. I was just about to get myself a coffee.'

'Erm. Where are you now?'

I was a little puzzled.

'I just told you, I'm by the harb...'

'No. Sorry Alice. Where at the harbour?'

'I'm sitting...standing, by a bench overlooking the river. Erm...there's a yacht moored in front of me; the *Amitié*.'

'I'll meet you there in about ten minutes. I just have one more call to make.'

'I'd really like to have that coffee Pascal.'

'We can go there afterwards. I need to talk to you privately first. Is that OK.'

Then I understood.

'Yes OK. I'll stay here. See you later.'

'Bye Alice.'

I don't know a great deal of French; but I recognised the word Amitié...friendship.

Fifteen or so minutes later, I saw Pascal walking towards me. He smiled warmly as he approached.

'OK?'

'Yes Pascal. Were your calls beneficial.'

He nodded.

'Yes. I think so.'

'Do you have a little more clarity now?'

'Yes. As you say, a little more, but there are gaps and...'

'Loose ends.'

He tipped his head towards his right shoulder questioningly.

'Yes. That is correct.'

'Can you tell me?'

'Of course Alice.' Contemplatively, he looked across the river. 'It is beautiful here isn't it.'

I nodded.

'Yes it is. It would be even better with a coffee,' I added tongue-in-cheek. I don't know why I do that.

When a situation should be viewed as thoughtful, I respond like a frivolous schoolgirl.

He turned and looked at me.

'Alice, I really think you are unique,' he replied with a smirk.

'Unique. I have never been accused of being unique before. That's a first,' I said, with a sincere smile.

He sat thoughtfully and then let out a sigh.

'My father's death wasn't an accident.'

That bombshell was sobering and removed instantly, any light-heartedness. Together we stared across the river. I, momentarily numbed…

'Witnesses said that the driver ran down my father as he crossed the road. The driver then drove off at speed. The police found the car on a derelict building site in another part of the city. It was burned out. Obviously, it was set on fire to remove any evidence.'

'He was *murdered*? It was a *deliberate* act?'

He sighed and nodded his head.

'I can't believe it Pascal. *Why*? *Why* would somebody kill him? I don't understand?'

'He told me that he was coming to meet you Alice. Did he say why?'

Not for the first time, my mind and thoughts were in a spiral. I thought for a few moments…

'We had met in the *Jardin des Plantes*.'

'Yes. I know that. What did he talk to you about?'

165

I wasn't sure what Pascal knew? How much his father had told him was unknown to me. So, I went over everything from my first meeting with him; to my last...

After I had finished, he sat deep in thought...

Throughout my recollections, he hadn't reacted to any of the conversation I'd had with his father. His expression was one of indifference. I don't know what I was expecting, but unresponsiveness was not it. Then he narrowed his eyes searchingly.

'Why did he arrange to meet you again at the Café le petit pont?'

'He said that he had more to tell me but that he had to go to meet with someone...or an appointment? I...can't remember exactly.'

'Please try to remember Alice; it could be important. Did he give an address or name of whom he was going to meet?'

I shook my head.

'No. He didn't. Sorry Pascal.'

Then I recalled the letter.

'He did say that he had written a erm...a summary I think, in a letter.'

'A letter?'

'Yes.'

'Do you have the letter?'

I shook my head.

'No. He never gave it to me. It was in his pocket, but, I guess with him being late for his appointment or whatever, he forgot to give it to me. I was hoping that he might bring it to the…' I pulled up short as I realised that to continue might have been, may be a little too upsetting for him.

He stared once again across the river.

'He did say that it contained something else of importance, that might explain things or the situation for me…something like that.'

He swung around and stared at me. His eyebrows were raised high and his expression searching and penetrating.

'He didn't say what it was?'

I shook my head.

'No. I'm sorry Pascal. He didn't,' I said apologetically.

He looked towards the ground, and in a whisper said, 'a letter?' and then repeated it,' a letter. Could it possibly be?' He stopped and looked across the river once again.

'Please excuse me Alice. I have to make another call.' He looked all around us and then took out his phone and pressed a number. The conversation in French went over my head, and other than the odd word or two, I understood nothing of its content.

He finished and ended the call. He placed his phone back into his pocket.

He looked at me absorbedly.

'The person I have just spoken with is a friend of the family that will be able to go through my father's clothing. I need to know what happened to the letter.'

I was a little perturbed to honest that he placed the urgency of the whereabouts of a letter of unknown content, above that of the need to know who his father's killer or killers were.

I think he sensed my uneasiness.

'That letter Alice, could be the reason my father was killed. I…we, need to know where it is?'

'We?'

He nodded and let out a sigh.

'If it is still in his pocket, then it can be retrieved. If, however, it is not on his person, then who has it? If the police have it, then it's content might be of great interest to…well. If the killer had another person nearby ready to remove the letter in the chaos that follows such a tragedy, then that could also be problematic for you.'

'*Me*?' I questioned once again.

'It will have your name on it, and as I suspect, you were already being observed by others.'

I guess I'd had enough…

'Right. What the *fuck* is going on?'

He looked at me sympathetically through kind and understanding eyes which made me feel a little guilty at snarling at someone who had just lost his father in what now transpires to be, criminal and evil circumstances, and who seems on the face of it, like me, to be an unwilling participant.

'I'm sorry Pascal.'

He reached out and held my hand.

'It is understandable Alice. You have been dragged into a situation not of your choosing and one that is out of your control. You are owed an explanation. You have been so trusting. I have to ask you to be the same; for just a little while longer. I have a friend who is coming down here to us. He can be trusted and he is…was, a good friend to my father. He is bringing with him, information that will hopefully, how you say, join the dots together.'

He shrugged his shoulders. 'Maybe not all, but…'

'Can I ask Pascal. How you know someone that is able to access your father's clothing? Does he work within the police?'

He thought for a moment…

'He is with the Gendarmerie. It is the military arm of the police. He has a lot of influence.'

'He is high up, high-ranking?'

He nodded.

'Yes. Very senior level.'

I think I already knew the answer to my next question.

'Is he part of the organisation that your father...' I stopped fleetingly. 'Do *you* belong to it Pascal?'

He stared at me nonchalantly.

'Yes. Yes, I am Alice.'

'As I said to you before, all your father told me about it, was that they...you, solve puzzles and tie up loose ends. Can I ask what it is? What puzzles do you solve? What are the loose ends?'

'When my friend arrives he may be able to tell you more. I am unable to. I'm sorry Alice, but it is for your protection.'

'Speaking of which. How much danger do you think I am in?'

'We will know more when he arrives. Until then...'

'Yes I know; be vigilant.'

He nodded.

'I am afraid so. I'm so sorry. Until we get more clarity. We just don't know presently.'

'I contacted my sister to tell her that I will be staying here a little while longer.'

Once again, he narrowed his eyes.

'You didn't tell her you were here in *Saint-Goustan*?'

I shook my head.

'No. I managed to think ahead a little.'

He smiled and nodded his head.

'I told her I was staying in Paris.' I paused briefly…
'Clever that Pascal.'

He looked confused.

'I don't understand?'

'Getting me to arrange another flight home, just on the off-chance, or likelihood that someone might know that I had changed it and turn up at the airport.'

He nodded and smiled.

'Loose ends Alice.'

I nodded.

'Indeed.'

'You can't be too careful. As I said, we are not absolutely sure what, or who, we are dealing with and how far their tentacles reach. There are, even for us, *too* many loose ends at the moment.'

'With so many loose ends seemingly trailing all over the place; do you ever trip over them?'

He smirked.

'I love your way of thinking Alice. Do you write the way you think?'

I raised my eyebrows. It was my time to offer him a grin.

He continued, 'I should read one of your books.'

'You mean you haven't?'

He smiled.

I looked at him meaningfully. Once again, I already knew the answer.

'Your friend that is coming; is he with your organisation?'

He nodded.

'Hmm.'

He smiled.

'He'll set sail first thing tomorrow morning.'

'Set sail?'

'Yes. He has a large yacht a little further around the coast where he lives. He is sailing it here to *Saint-Goustan*. Then we can get you safely back home to the UK.' He gave me a reassuring smile. 'Coffee?'

I smiled and nodded.

'Yes please.'

We both stood. He in the belief that I would be out of the frame by tomorrow, and I knowing that this little part of the puzzle, that would be *me* then, has no intention of slinking back to the UK without knowing just what I have been, or *still am*, involved in. Reasons: One, I don't want to place my family in jeopardy. Two, that distinctive characteristic of mine that lends itself to the unrelenting need to be curious, and three, the urge to prolong my life for as long as is possible!

CHAPTER SEVENTEEN

Sunday 16th April 2023
19:42
Saint-Goustan

As sure as he could be, Pascal had thought it safe enough to dine out. He was quite certain that the friend that owned the house could not be associated with him, his father or the organisation to which he was a subscriber. We were both famished to be honest as we had eaten very little since the layby; the baguette and shared cake from the supermarket. He chose a wonderfully located restaurant, the L'Armoric. It sits on the banks of the Rivière d'Auray on a small "Y" shaped promontory where the river flows under a medieval stone bridge.

'Is this OK Alice?'

I smiled.

'I think this will do just fine.'

The waiter came across to the table and laid out the menus. He leaned over to us as if passing a secret.

'If I may suggest, the filet de Dorade and filet de Boeuf are particularly good this evening. But please take your time to choose.'

He smiled graciously, turned and walked over to another table.

I suspected that the seemingly inside information, was passed to all the customers in the restaurant on instruction from the chef.

We didn't really speak much; we studied the menus and a few minutes later the waiter reappeared.

'Are you ready to order?'

We both nodded and gave our preferences.

Pascal looked at me.

'Wine?'

I nodded and smiled effortlessly.

He picked up the wine list and looked at me once again.

'Red…and you choose.'

The waiter wrote down the selected wine and with the same gracious smile, turned and headed first to the bar area to give the wine order to the bartender, then off towards the kitchen.

174

'How are you Alice?'

I know what he was asking.

'I'm still so confused about it all.'

With recognition that we both had to be careful what we spoke about in public even though Pascal thought we were in a safe place; we had both moved into a covert approach of conversation.

'I'm sure it will be better tomorrow Alice.'

I smiled.

'Let's hope so Pascal.'

He smiled and looked at me. His smile and demeanour felt different. It was honest and warm which I had felt from him previously, but this time his smile and his eyes were saying something else…something deeper, and he knew that it had touched me with tenderness. I was not expecting it, and it had taken me by surprise to be honest. I leaned back into my chair and looked at him and he at me.

'Well,' I said impishly. 'What about that.'

He sat back and laughed.

The meal was a delight and afterwards we walked back to the house, his arm around my shoulder and mine around his waist. I had been taken aback by the suddenness of an unexpected romance, especially arriving as it had, in the middle of such a turbulent and tragic time. I hadn't had a boyfriend or partner if you wish, for quite a while. I was too busy writing, and to be truthful, I wasn't bothered either way. I had thought about a dating site, but I felt that I didn't want to display myself in a shop window. Not that I am against them, a couple of my friends have developed good relationships through them, but it's not my bag.

Having said all that, and regardless of Brexit, it didn't take much effort to slide under his duvet…and as with the meal earlier, I was ready for it, and it was absolutely delicious.

CHAPTER EIGHTEEN

Monday 17th April 2023
09:51
Saint-Goustan

Knocking on the front door awakened us. We turned and looked at each other; my eyes wide and showing a little apprehension.

'It's OK Alice. It will be my friend.' He leaned slowly across to my face and kissed me tenderly on the lips. He moved his head away.

'Are you OK Alice. Is everything alright?'

I think he meant the sleeping together - although there hadn't been much of that going on, and not the situation we found ourselves in.

I smiled affectionately.

'Yes. Everything is just fine Pascal.'

He smiled. I continued, 'You can wait on my table, anytime.'

His smile rescinded to a rascally grin.

Another knock came to the door…this time a little more audible and meaningful.

'*Merde!*'

He leapt out of bed revealing a rather nice bum. He slipped on his boxers and went downstairs. The question is often asked, "did the Earth move?" when most of the time, the *bed* hardly moves. The bed mattress last night was well and truly tested!

I climbed out of the bed and as I did so, a dark thought came to me, what if it wasn't his friend and we had been discovered. I dressed as quickly as I could and rushed down the stairs.

As I reached the bottom stair I saw a well-groomed man who I'd say looked to be in his mid-forties hugging Pascal. I stopped and stood still not wanting to interrupt the moment.

He looked at me, then to Pascal, still in his boxers and then back to me with my hair all over the map. It didn't take a genius to work out the sleeping arrangements. He sat down at the dining table. With his index finger, Pascal gently moved away the few tears that lay heavy in his eyelids and then walked to the kitchen sink.

The man gave me a knowing, yet courteous smile.

'Good morning Alice.'

'Alice this is Pierre,' said Pascal without turning around.

I returned an equally shrewd smile.

'Nice to meet you Pierre. I wish it was in better circumstances. Pascal turned and smiled warmly.

Pierre nodded.

'Indeed Alice. Indeed.'

Pascal walked across to the table carrying a freshly made cafetiere. Once again, the aroma filled the air.

He poured us out a coffee, walked over to the work surface, placed it on the top.

'If you could excuse me for a moment. I'll just slip a shirt and jeans on.' He went upstairs. Pierre and I just looked at each other; unspoken across the table.

On the table were a selection of breads, cheeses and croissants and we both began to tuck in.

Pascal came back into the kitchen and sat down with us at the table.

'How was your journey here Pierre?' asked Pascal

'It was a good sail.' He turned and looked at me; it was an odd stare that was unconcerned, yet penetrating. He then turned away and looked at Pascal.

'I am so sorry my friend.'

Pascal nodded acquiescently.

'It came as such a shock Pierre. I was unprepared.'

Pierre returned an accepting nod.

'I know. I know. How can you prepare for something like that?'

'Do you have any news on who it might have been Pierre?'

'No.'

We sat silently momentarily. Then Pascal broke the silence.

'Could it have been to do with the letter?'

Pierre's stare became intense and concentrated. His eyes narrowed questioningly.

'What letter?'

Pascal looked at me.

'At my meeting with him at the Jardin, Benoît told me that he had a letter with him that outlined what he had told me about my genealogy, but also that it containing something important or significant, or both. I can't quite remember.'

'Do you have the letter?'

I looked at Pascal.

'My father died before he could give it to her.'

'He had it with him?'

'We believe so.'

I continued, 'he asked me to meet him for dinner at Café le petit pont later that evening. I presumed he was brining it with him.'

'Where is the letter now Pascal?'

He shook his head.

'I don't know. I have made a call to…' he paused and looked at me, '…a friend who might be able discover its whereabouts. I am hopeful.'

180

'Please tell me the moment you know anything Pascal.'

I was looking from one to the other. A certain amount of trepidation had just let itself in through the front door. I should have felt a little put out that he clearly didn't wish to give away the name of his friend. On the other hand, in the current situation, it might be better that I didn't know.

Once again the probing look from Pierre.

'Excuse me Pierre, but I can't help noticing that you keep staring a little intensely at me. It is, if I may say, a little disconcerting.'

His stare became a mischievous grin.

'Hmm. I can see that you are plainspoken, Alice.'

'Well, you know. It saves time doesn't it.'

His eyebrows raised and his waggish appearance was replaced by a cheerier smile.

'Indeed it does.'

I leaned forwards, picked up my coffee took a sip and sat back in my chair.

'Utterly to die for.' Then in horror I realised what I had rather *stupidly* and inappropriately said. I turned and looked at Pascal apologetically.

He smiled warmly at me, releasing any guilt from my remark.

I returned a heartfelt smile.

'Alice.'

I turned.

'Yes Pierre?'

'Would you please go over everything that Benoît discussed with you.'

I let out a deep sigh.

'Do you mean from the *very* first time we met?'

'No. I know about that.'

I raised my eyebrows.

'Why am I not surprised?'

He smiled.

'If you could tell me what he told you the last time you met with him; is that possible Alice? It could be important.'

'Well it was rather a lot. I'm not sure that I can repeat it verbatim; word for word.'

'What ever you can remember; it *may* be helpful.'

I recounted the conversation I'd had with Benoît. I think I managed to include most things that he told me. It was quite painful talking about a conversation with someone, whom is no longer with us.

Both Pascal and Pierre clearly needed time to absorb what I had said: Pascal, more so I think, as it was the last conversation that anyone had with his father, other than the person or persons he had the appointment with and whose conversation would probably never be known. And I of course, was presuming that he hadn't spoken with Pascal after my meeting.

Pierre broke the silence…
'What you were told is not all strictly true Alice.'
Oh no. Not again, I thought to myself; yet more misinformation and half-truths.
Pierre stared at him attentively. Not for the first time since depositing my book at Shakespeare and Company, I was utterly muddled.
'What do you mean Pierre?' asked Pascal.
Pierre let out a sigh.
'OK so. Alice. Your ancestry is correct. Your family came from the de Merclesden line. With Robert and Alice in the time of the slaughter of Béziers.' He smiled, 'history repeating itself with names. After the adoption of Thomas, you became Rochambeau. And the rest you know. However, *your* genealogy Pascal, is slightly different in the fact that your ancestor did not join the pact made by Thomas and Hugh de Rochambeau at a *later* date; he in fact was Amaury de Rochambeau, the brother of Hugh de Rochambeau, whose family name and decent later changed to…Lavigne. The oath was pledged, and the pact made by them all, at its commencement…the beginning.'
I didn't know about them, but I *really* had to think about that one.

Pascal stared down at the tabletop. Then, at the same moment, the realisation occurred to us both. He looked up directly at me. Although not related by blood, we were absolutely connected. Our ancestors knew each other. Not only that, they shared a vow and a vision of seeking the truth.

'All those years ago Pascal.'

He shook his head.

'It is quite unbelievable.'

I let out a sigh.

'Serendipity.'

Pierre continued, 'so you Alice, are de Merclesden who became Rochambeau, and you Pascal are Rochambeau who became Lavigne. It's really quite extraordinary.'

Pascal's mobile rang out. He looked at the number and then accepted the call.

He spoke in French, and yet again the conversation went right over my head. I could see from his expression and body language that it wasn't good news. The fact that he was taking the call in Pierre's presence told me that it was about the current situation. He ended the call and looked at Pierre.

Pierre exhaled meaningfully.

'We have to find it Pascal.'

I put two and two together.

'The letter is missing?'

Pascal looked at me and nodded.

'It was not in his clothing.'

Then it occurred to me.

'He might have changed his jacket. That's a possibility…isn't it?'

Pascal looked at Pierre. He reached for his phone and made a call. After a few words had been exchanged, he looked at me.

'Can you remember what jacket he was wearing?'

I nodded.

'Yes. It was a light grey with different brightly coloured cuff buttons. Four on each I think.'

He spoke to the person on the phone. Once again I could see disappointment etched in his face.

'It was the same jacket.'

'It could have fallen out of his pocket when…' I checked myself from continuing.

'I don't think so. The police arrived very quickly. In Paris, the police are never very far away. They cordoned off the area.'

'I agree with Alice,' said Pierre. It could have fallen out and someone may have retrieved it.'

They looked at each other.

'Or…'

'I know Pascal.'

I was guessing that the "I know" was what was suggested by Pascal. Either someone intercepted it or someone in the police have it in their possession, for whatever reason.

185

'Have you *any* idea what the letter might contain Pierre?' I asked.

He shook his head.

'Benoît didn't mention the letter to me. I just didn't know. But, whatever it contains, must be of great importance.'

I don't know why, and don't know for certain, but I had the feeling that he knew something more.

Pierre looked at Pascal once again with a meaningful gaze.

'I have something to tell you Pascal and...' he looked at me, and turned back to Pascal, '...with Alice being in the middle of all this somehow,' he looked at me again and then back to Pascal, 'as you are well aware, your father played a significant and crucial part in our organisation.' One again he looked at me, 'Alice, Benoît told you of another organisation, a brotherhood connected to the time of Béziers and maybe they existed before that time; who knows?'

I nodded.

'*Défenseur de la Foi* – Defender of the faith.'

Pierre smiled.

'Yes. Or, *Fidei defensor* as they were also known. Your father Pascal, knew a lot more than we know about them.'

Pascal looked totally mystified.

'I don't understand Pierre?'

I did.

'Pascal, your father was *Défenseur de la Foi*. Am I right Pierre?'

He shook his head slowly.

'No. He wasn't an associate, but he was a bridge between our organisation, and their, for want of a better word, brotherhood. Although brotherhood might not be strictly true as I am led to believe that women have been affiliates throughout its history.'

Pascal shook his head.

'That's *impossible*. I would have known. He would have *told me*.' He seemed perturbed and upset.

Pierre continued, 'you have to understand that you having knowledge of our organisation alone, places you is some danger. However, if you knew everything about your father...the risk of harm and vulnerability increases significantly.'

'So why tell me now. Are you not putting me in the very danger you have avoided?'

'Circumstances dictate: an event or an occurrence can change everything. We don't know what is happening right now. And with the cruel death of your father...you have a right to know. I don't know how much he knew? As I said, too much information can be unsafe.'

I thought it time for some clarity for me.

'What is the name of your organisation?'

Pierre looked at me apologetically.

'I cannot tell you that Alice.'

'Well that's just dandy.'

'Dandy?'

I looked at him as the sentiment landed.

'Dandy…oh yes, I see.'

'I know *all this,* and now I have just found out that I am connected to all of, *this,* and yet you can't give me the name of it.'

He looked at me apologetically.

'I'm afraid it would not be in your best interest Alice; and quite possibly…ours also.'

'I don't *believe* this! I'm up to my neck in god knows what, dating back to, god knows when, and you can't give me a…' I took a moment and let out a sigh. 'Oh never mind.' I leaned forward and took another sip of coffee. It gave me a moment in which to sit back, get off my high horse and put the whole thing into perspective. Pascal's father had just been murdered and I was stressing about a name.

'I'm sorry Pascal. It was selfish of me. I should have been more thoughtful.'

He shook his head.

'It's OK Alice. Really it is. I understand.' He looked at Pierre. '*We* have involved Alice Pierre. She has a *right* to know.'

Pierre looked at me regretfully.

'I am sorry Alice. But at this moment, until we have some clarity, all we can do is to keep you safe, and get you home to your family. We feel that you are an innocent party and will not be directly threatened.'

I leaned forward and raised my eyebrows as if in disclosure.

'Has it occurred to you Pierre. That Benoît might have been murdered...' I stopped and looked at Pascal apologetically, but continued as I thought it could be relevant and place me, not on the periphery, but at the centre of what was happening, '...to prevent him giving the letter, to *me*?'

They looked at each other. I might have read it wrong, but I didn't believe it had occurred to them. And that really surprised me. Maybe it's because I write this "stuff" for a living; but to me at least, it *has* to be a scenario. I think that they were so wrapped up in whatever it is that their organisation does, and trying to unravel the situation, as they understand it to be; that they didn't see that particular consequence coming; wood for the trees and all that. I was astonished to be honest. It was obvious to me.

'There then,' I said a little too self-confidently and possibly a little inappropriately, and settled back into my chair.

I left it there...for the present at least. The three of us sat there in quietude. Each of us lost in our own thoughts and contemplations...

189

Then Pierre punctuated the silence.

'There *is* more I can tell you Alice.'

'Oh. OK.'

'It concerns your great grandfather George.'

'*George*?' I had to think and catch up on my more immediate ancestors rather than the medieval.

'OK George. He was in the SOE during World War Two and got himself put into jail to meet up with…'

Just then in another eye-opener, and looking at Pascal's face, the realisation hit both of us again, simultaneously.

'*I know*!' he said in surprise.

'My Great grandfather and your great grandfather Pascal. Again, our two families met together in time.'

'*Extraordinary*!' he exclaimed. In the middle-ages, World War Two…' he looked at me, '…and now.'

'Do you think they knew that they were…had been associated in the past?' I pondered.

We both looked at Pierre. The look on his face clearly told us, that if he knew, he wasn't saying.

'Shall I continue?' said Pierre

We both nodded.

'Benoît told you Alice, that George's reason for coming to France during the war, was to find out who was betraying the French Jewish résistance fighters, and that the SOE believed it to be the communists. It wasn't the entire reason.'

I let out a deep sigh.

'Here we go again.'

'Pascal, as you know from your father's book, your Great grandfather, Jean whom was thirty-one in nineteen forty-two, was the man held in jail for committing a petty theft. He didn't commit any offence. The SOE had planted a stolen gold watch, which they had arranged to be stolen, in Jean's house and informed the local police. He was arrested and held in jail.'

Pascal looked a little puzzled.

'That's not what my father said in his book?'

Pierre nodded.

'I know. He said many things in his book that were not true. He wrote it that way to mislead and misinform.'

'I don't understand Pierre? His book is based on lies?'

'Not really Pascal. A few deceptions to deter further investigations by others.'

'Others?'

'Yes. Again, it was to keep people safe.'

Clearly he wasn't going to expand any further.

'It was imperative that Jean was in the custody of the police on a civil matter, keeping him out of the way of the Gestapo; temporarily at least.'

'So, being arrested allowed George to make contact with him?' I said.

He nodded.

'Yes.'

'But I thought that George didn't make contact?' questioned Pascal. Then he realised, 'But that was also a lie, wasn't it?'

Pierre nodded.

'Alice, Pascal. I have quite a story to tell you. Would you like to hear that story?'

We both nodded expectantly...

CHAPTER NINETEEN

Monday 17th August 1942
00:37
36 kilometres from Paris

No sooner had the single engine Lysander landed; it was airborne again on a heading for England.

Momentarily, George stood silently in the field before heading towards a wooded area.
A flashlight caught him in its beam followed by a female voice.

'Cognoscere hostem tuum.'
'Non sum inimicus tuus,' he replied.
The light was extinguished and lit by moonlight a young woman's face appeared in front of his. She smiled.
'I am Yvette.'
He nodded.

'I'm George.'

She gave him a waggish grin.

'What?' he asked.

'You are very attractive.'

'This isn't a date.'

She smiled once again and shrugged her shoulders.

'I was expecting...I don't know. We must leave now.'

She turned and he followed dutifully behind. He watched her as she strode purposely towards the woodland; a Sten gun slung across her back over a soft pink merino wool jumper tucked into a pair of black slacks and on her head; a black beret, suggested to him, the very notion of a French female resistance fighter.

Very little was said during the drive to Paris. It took several hours, as she had to take a safe route around the German checkpoints by using little used lanes. At one point they left the car they were in outside a barn; she placed her Sten gun in the car boot.

They walked across a field to a farmhouse and climbed into another car: the keys ready and waiting for her in the dashboard; they set off once again...

After the potentially hazardous journey, they arrived in the outskirts of Paris, it was 03:57. She parked the car outside a tenement block. She got out of the car, looking furtively around her she beckoned him out. They walked to a semi-pedestrianized area. He looked up at the street name, Rue Saint-Séverin, it is within the 5th arrondissement of Paris. On the right hand side of the street, they walked by a restaurant that during the day would be occupied mainly by Germans. A little further on, she stopped at a door of a substantial stone built building. There were deep first and second floor French windows each with its own balcony and ornate, wrought ironwork railings. She placed the key into the lock and opened the door. He followed quickly behind. Through another door off to the right, they entered her apartment; George closed the door behind him. She switched on the light.

She placed the keys on the kitchen table, took off her beret, hung it up on a coat hook, turned and looked at George, smiled and nodded.

'Hmm. Even better in the light.'

George raised his eyebrows. He couldn't be drawn away from the fact that he found her attractive. Of course her prettiness would not distract him from what he had come to do. Well, a little diversion maybe.

She held up a cup.

'Coffee? Or maybe you would like to sleep after your journey?'

He was wide-awake. Training as a SOE operative involved much sleep deprivation. It had become the norm for him.

He smiled.

'Coffee would be good.'

With the coffee made, she carried a cafetiere over to the table, and poured out two cups. It was the first time he had sensed such an aroma.

'That smells wonderful.'

He lifted it to his nose and then took a sip.

'Sublime.'

She smiled playfully.

'Me, or the coffee?'

He smiled.

'We have a job to do Yvette.'

She nodded and smiled impishly.

'I know. I know.'

He returned a wry smile.

'OK. Tell me the situation.'

'I am Jean's sister.'

'I see. I didn't know that.'

She smiled.

'It is best that we only know what we should.'

He nodded.

'Where is Jean being held?'

'He is in the headquarters of the police. It is not far from here.'

'I have to speak to him as soon as I can. But firstly, I have to deal with Maurice Duclos.'

She looked intensely at him.

Her facial expression became penetrating.

'He is *filth*!'

'Well, his time is nearly done.'

'He is responsible for the betrayal of many innocent French Jews that have been fighting alongside us for our cause and struggle to rid ourselves of the Nazis. I *hate* the Communists.'

I held her arm.

'It will end. I promise Yvette.'

She looked kindly at him.

'Thank you for coming. We do appreciate it.'

He smiled.

'I wouldn't have missed this coffee for all the world.'

She returned a warm smile.

'And meeting me of course.'

'Well that goes without saying.'

'Still, you could mention it if you like,' she said with a schoolgirl grin.

'Hmm.'

'Where are we at the moment with regards to Duclos?'

'We know where he meets with his Gestapo contact. We have managed to set up a meeting between them. A note was given to Duclos, which seemingly was written by his German *pig* friend, asking that they meet tomorrow at 23:00.'

He looked penetratingly at her.

'Can you do this Yvette?'

'I have lost good and kind friends through these two *pigs*. Can I do this? The only thing that I fear is, that my ecstasy interferes with my aim.'

He looked at her. Although well briefed before he left for France, he hadn't really taken into consideration or understood the depth of feeling, the hatred and hunger for revenge that had gripped the French people.

He nodded.

'I understand Yvette.'

An expression of doubt set across her face. However, it was replaced by a genuine and honest smile.

'What is the plan Yvette?'

She explained the assassination plot - which is in reality was what it was going to be - and then went over it again to make sure that he had understood clearly. He had.

'What about reprisals?' he asked.

198

She let out a significant sigh.

'I don't think that there will be. It will look like they have shot each other...it happens all the time here, even though the Gestapo may have suspicions, I don't think that they will act, as it might draw too much attention to the fact that Duclos was working and informing on French citizens for them. As you say, they usually round up innocent people for a firing squad in retaliation. But I believe that they will want to keep the arrangement they had between them, quiet. Perhaps, to find another source, and continue with their sickening deceits.'

'Another traitor you mean?'

She nodded.

'Yes.'

'Hmm.'

'It is a gamble I agree. But it *has* to be done. He *has* to pay for what he has done. It cannot wait for the end of the war. This must be settled now.'

He nodded once again in agreement...

CHAPTER TWENTY

Tuesday 18th August 1942
22:30

Yvette and George had arrived early at the rendezvous point as Yvette thought that the Gestapo officer might check out the area first. The Gestapo were suspicious of their own shadows. They were parked out of view in a passageway; hidden, but in sight of where Duclos and the officer would meet. She was right, at 22: 47 the officer pulled up in his staff car. He got out and looked all around him attentively, scrutinising every corner, every house, every car…every shadow.

Duclos arrived. The coast was clear for them to make their move stealthily. George and Yvette had to move quickly before their deception was uncovered. They came upon them, with their pistols pointing at them, and told them to raise their arms and move into an alleyway. Yvette quickly searched

Duclos and removed his pistol. Then George removed the Luger from the officer's holster. Duclos and the officer were in a stunned shock at the swiftness of what was unfurling, that they didn't have time to think. Yvette pointed the Luger at Duclos's head and pulled the trigger. At the same time, George levelled Duclos's gun at the officer's heart and pulled his trigger. Both fell to the ground simultaneously. They quickly placed Duclos's gun and the Gestapo officer's luger into their recipient's hands; and they fled. As they got into the car, they heard a police whistle. The police officer was a patriot working with the résistance and was a part of the plan. He would also be a witness later, to what had happened. He would say that he had heard two men shouting, and as he turned the corner he witnessed the officer and Duclos shoot and kill each other.

Yvette drove the car slowly back to her flat. Once inside, and without speaking a word, she opened a bottle of red wine and poured out two glasses. She held hers up.

'For those of our friends that have been taken too soon.'

George raised his glass also, and nodded quiescently.

They both took a big slug of wine and sat down together at the table.

Yvette looked at him purposely and longingly.

'We make love now George.'

He gave her a waggish grin…

CHAPTER TWENTY-ONE

Wednesday 19th August 1942
08:27
Rue Saint-Séverin

George turned and looked at Yvette. A shaft of early morning sunlight shining through the large French window, gave a soft, silky sheen to her hair. He looked at her face; there was an air of contentment and peace. Slowly, she opened her eyes. Lovingly, she smiled at him. She leaned over to him and kissed him tenderly on his lips.

'Good morning George.'

He smiled affectionately.

'Good morning Yvette. Coffee?'

She smiled broadly and nodded.

He climbed out of bed; dressed and made his way through to the kitchen.

She joined him in the kitchen/dining area. The air once again suffused with the aroma of freshly made coffee. She drew out a chair and sat down opposite him. She placed her elbows on the table and rested her chin in the palms of her hands.

'It's amazing what you can accomplish in 24 hours.' She smirked.

He laughed.

She smiled and nodded her head assuredly.

They sat silently briefly; looking at each other and also each contemplating the next act. This was the true reason that George had clandestinely arrived in France.

'OK Yvette. How is it to happen?

'The police officer that helped us with Duclos, came up with the plan to have Jean arrested and placed into custody before *Werner Dreschsler, could get to him.'

'What does the police officer know Yvette?'

'Only what he has to.'

'He doesn't know why your brother has to be kept safe?'

She shook her head.

'No.'

'Werner Dreschsler. Who is he and how did he discover what Jean has?'

'Werner Dreschsler, is a Chief Gestapo officer and Heinrich Himmler's deputy of affairs of the Ahnenerbe in matters of the Aryan race, ancestry and the occult. They are obsessed with the mystical and the creation of a pure Germanic ethnicity.'

George nodded.

'How much does Dreschsler know?'

She shrugged her shoulders and shook her head.

'We don't know George. We don't know.'

He looked at her meaningfully.

'What do *you* know Yvette?'

'I don't know the information or knowledge that Jean has. You know how it works George. He alone knows…and that's it.'

He nodded.

'When?'

'Tomorrow. We can't risk leaving it any longer. They will soon discover where Jean is and…well. It *has* to be tomorrow.'

Once again he acknowledged her with an affirming nod of the head.

'Jean will be released at 06:00. We will pick him up and drive to the railway station, the Gare de Lyon for Béziers. I have tickets and passes for us all. We have to change just once, which is from the same station.'

'How long is the journey altogether Yvette?'

'If all runs smoothly, it's about six hours. Tomorrow afternoon, Dreschsler will receive news that Jean has been seen in Béziers. He will leave immediately.'

'By train?'

She shook her head.

'There are no trains to Béziers in the afternoon. He will use his staff car. His driver will drive him there. He will arrive in the early hours of Friday morning.'

'When Dreschsler arrives he will receive information that Jean is meeting with a contact. Dreschsler will be there.'

'You're sure.'

She nodded with certainty.

'I am *certain*. Himmler desperately wants what Jean has.' Again she nodded. 'He will be there.'

'Where is the rendezvous?'

'Dio Castle. It is an abandoned 12th century citadel in the village of Dio-et-Valquières. It's about one hour's drive from the centre of Béziers.'

'How are we to get there?'

'There will be a car waiting for us at the station. We will later be met by…a friend.'

'A brotherhood friend Yvette?'

She shook her head.

'No. A trusted and loyal friend. If all goes well, she will drive us as close as she can to the castle where we will wait. We have to arrive much earlier. We must be ready for Dreschsler's arrival.'

'Weapons?'

'They are already hidden along with everything else we need, at the castle along with a freshly dug pit for the bodies.'

George nodded. Any feelings of remorse or guilt had to be abandoned. The situation, importance and circumstances, could not allow any judgments to be clouded by responsibility or self-reproach. They had a job to do. And the business was of the *utmost* importance.

'And afterwards?'

'It is about two to three hours to the border of Spain. We will drive to a small village, which is about an hour's drive from the castle. We then have to walk. This will be the most dangerous and hazardous part of the journey. Once again, if all goes well, we will be met near the border by the Spanish resistance, and cross into the safety of Spain.'

'There's a lot of, "if all goes well" Yvette.' He smiled.

She laughed.

'As always George.'

'What if Himmler sends more soldiers to support Dreschsler?'

She shook her head.

'No. He is cautious. I think he wants to keep this as secretive as he can. I don't even think Hitler knows exactly what Himmler is up to.'

George raised his eyebrows. He seemed a little surprised. She continued, 'No. I think it will just be him and his driver.'

'If all goes well.'

She laughed.

'Exactly!'

George understood why he had only just been told about the preparations and actions: if he had been captured before meeting Yvette, or if something had gone wrong; he didn't have any vital information that could be extracted under interrogation. It was safer all round for the preservation of lives and of the mission. One detail however, was puzzling him.

'Why are we not just taking Jean from the police station straight to Spain? Why this elaborate and dangerous route?'

She hesitated momentarily…

'It has to be known that Jean is dead.'

'Jean…dead? I don't understand Yvette?'

'If we take Jean to Spain, Dreschsler will continue to hunt down…even in Spain. He will *never* give up. It is too important to them. There are many German sympathisers in Spain. They are unknown to us.'

'So?'

'So. We have to make Himmler believe that Jean is dead and Dreschsler's driver was a traitor to their cause. He will then try to pursue him. But he will fail; because he will be dead also.'

George sat back into his chair. She continued, 'It's all about deception isn't it George. That's the nature of our business and always has been; as with Duclos's death. Dreschsler's driver is about the same height and weight as Jean. We have a copy of Jean's Identity card which has been partially burned, but still decipherable.'

'Burned?'

'Yes. Dreschsler will be shot as will his driver. His driver will be dressed in spare clothing of Jean's. The bodies will be burned: Dreschsler enough to still be recognised, and his driver, in a way that disguises and disfigures his face, partial body and his hands to eliminate any chance of fingerprints or physical identification. The staff car will be disposed of. And if questions are asked, friends in the village will say that they saw a uniformed German, driving the car at speed, away from the village. The villagers have a *hatred* of the Germans because of what they did there.'

'What was it they did Yvette?'

'It is of no concern at the moment George. The important issue is that the driver will be recognised as the traitor; that he has deceived Dreschsler and ultimately, Himmler. Of course being who he is, Himmler will suspect all is not as it seems; he will be sceptical, but will not have the proof to support his suspicion. He will be compelled to search for the driver. It happens. People's greed, desire for power, wealth and knowledge, can turn the loyalist of friends, into treacherous enemies.'

'What about the fire? Will it not draw attention?'

She shook her head.

'No. Farmers quite often burn agricultural waste products in the hillsides.'

George looked at Yvette. She looked so beautiful and demure. Underneath was this shrewd killer. It sent a slight chill down his spine. Either through his facial expression or just body language, she seemed to sense what he must have been thinking. She smiled broadly.

'It's OK George. You're safe enough. You are one of us.'

'If all goes well.'

She laughed.

'I am not, how do you say it, a black widow. I don't make love, then kill the person.'

He smiled…somewhat in relief.

She continued, 'however, I can make love, and then kill Nazi's.'

'Just Nazi's?'

'Not all Germans are Nazi's George. Not all of them. I'm convinced that there are many who would give up their weapons and return home to their families and loved ones…tomorrow if they could. Just like the rest of us caught up in that megalomaniac's vision of World order.'

He raised his eyebrows. He was a little taken aback. The last thing; the *very* last thing he expected, was an understanding of human nature in this sense at least, and albeit not forgiveness, there was in her voice, a tolerance. It made him aware of just how complex she was.

He leaned across the table, and with a loving smile beckoned her to reach out to him, where across the table, they kissed passionately.

The rest of the day was spent in going over the plan, eating and making love...

CHAPTER TWENTY-TWO

Thursday 20th August 1942
05:58
Rue Saint-Séverin,
Outside the Police station

The police station door opened and Jean stood in the doorway. He looked cautiously around him before spotting Yvette in the car. He released an affectionate smile and walked over to her. He looked inside and glimpsed George sat on the back seat. He released another smile and nodded his head in a contented greeting. He opened the door and got into the car.

Yvette gave him a loving hug, and then drove off towards the railway station.

'Jean, this is George.'

He turned around and put out his hand. George reciprocated and shook it firmly.

'It is good to meet you George. Thank you for coming. It is appreciated,' he said echoing the same words of his sister Yvette.

He looked at Yvette's eyes through the rear view mirror. There was an impishness radiating from them. He smiled.

'It is my pleasure Jean... believe me.'

They arrived at the railway station. Yvette parked the car and they got out. Although early, the station was surprisingly busy. It was helpful; as they were able to blend into the crowd. There were a few German soldiers dotted about, but the majority hadn't yet arrived. A little later, and it would be crawling with them. Yvette looked up at the station clock. 06:32. She looked for the platform that their train was to leave from. Just as she looked up at the board, a voice came from behind her.

'Papers!'

Calmly she turned around to face a German soldier. She reached inside her bag and pulled out her Identity card and travel papers. He scrutinised them, then her, then the I D and papers once again.

'Bag.'

She didn't protest. She opened her bag. He searched through it, then handed her papers back.

He nodded and gave her a small yet meaningful smile.

214

'Merci.'

She nodded. Maybe he was one of the Germans that Yvette had talked about yesterday; one that would rather be at home with his family, than stood on a railway platform in the early hours of the morning in a foreign country, where the locals hated them. As he walked away he looked over to George. Jean had gone to the kiosk to buy a morning paper. Without looking at the soldier, George walked over to Yvette, hugged her and kissed her. The soldier turned, and walked away. Jean walked over to them.

'OK?'

They both nodded.

'Platform 3,' said Yvette. 'The train is at the platform. We should go.'

The train pulled out of the station on time at 06:52.

After changing trains, and a wait of only 10 minutes before their connection; they continued their onward journey to *Béziers*.

They arrived in *Béziers* at 13:12. After having their tickets checked, they left the station building and walked over to a parking bay. Yvette looked around her. Then nodded and pointed to a car.

'There.'

215

They walked over to the car; Yvette opened the door. Pulled down the sun visor where a key fell onto the seat. They climbed into the car, she started the engine and they began their journey towards the village of Dio-et-Valquières. Yvette turned off the road and onto a dirt track. At the end of it was farmhouse. As they approached the farmhouse a young woman in her twenties appeared at the doorway and waved. Yvette got out of the car first. Smiling, she walked over to the young woman and hugged her.

Jean and George followed behind.

Jean also gave her a hug.

'George, this is Sylvie.'

George put out his hand as did she and they shook.

'It is nice to meet you George,' she said casting a knowing raised eyebrow to Yvette, where Yvette sported a playful smile. 'Hmm.'

George seemed a little uncertain what the "Hmm" meant.

'It's nice to meet you too Sylvie. I wish it could be in better circumstances.' He looked around him. 'It is so beautiful here.'

She smiled contentedly and nodded.

'Yes it is George.'

He looked behind him; sat high on a hilltop was the castle. A cold chill ran through him at what was to take place there.

216

'Is everything in readiness Sylvie?' asked Jean.

She nodded.

'Everything is in place.'

He nodded.

'That is good.'

'I have prepared a little food. Come.'

They followed her around the gable end of the house to the back garden. A table was groaning with food.

'A *little* food Sylvie?' She laughed and continued, 'We don't see food like this in Paris. Not in this quantity.'

Sylvie unfurled her arm.

'Come. Sit down.'

At the table she poured out the wine and sat down with the others. She raised her glass.

'To peace.'

They all raised their glasses and echoed her sentiment.

After a short time of eating and a little more wine, Yvette asked Sylvie, 'Where's your father Sylvie?'

He's out in the fields with the sheep.' She pointed to the hillside below the castle escarpment. 'Somewhere over there.' She laughed. 'I think he prefers his sheep to people.'

'He knows what is to happen?' asked George.

217

'Yes,' replied Sylvie. She looked at Yvette and Jean. I had a brother, Jules. He was a beautiful soul. Last April, nearby to here, a passing car was carrying a gestapo officer; he was shot and killed. Jules was in the village trading vegetables in the market. The Germans rounded up ten men; one of which was Jules. They took them to the church and held them there. After posting what they were going to do; they executed them the following day in the market square.'

Jean and Yvette hung their heads. George, although not surprised at the reprisal and ensuing atrocity, was clearly saddened.

'I am so sorry Sylvie. I have no words.'

'I have one George. Vengeance.'

The conversations became less fraught and more good-humoured as the day progressed to night. They turned in early, as the following day would be long and arduous.

A little later, through his bedroom window, George heard a man whistling a tuneful melody. It was Sylvie's father returning from his sheep in the hills. With Sylvie's brother still in mind, and the barbarity of what had occurred, his thoughts turned towards the act that was to play out. If he had in his mind any doubt or feelings of uncertainty…they had been usurped by the need for, "vengeance".

CHAPTER TWENTY-THREE

Friday 21st August 1942
09:27
Castle Dio
Dio-et-Valquières

Gestapo officer, Werner Dreschsler had, as anticipated, taken the bait and set off from Paris immediately with his driver at 17:00 the previous day. They had arrived at the village at 23:42 and found a lodging. Previously, the message that he had received from a trusted source, although unknown to him, wasn't as trusted as he thought, was that Jean would be at the castle at 11:00 hours.

At the castle, Yvette, Jean and George arranged and prepared themselves for Drechsler's arrival.

'Are you OK George?' asked Yvette.

'Yes. I am clear as to what is to be done.'

She held him tightly.

'You are a good man George.'

'As are you...not a good man, but...well...you know.'

She laughed.

'*Shhh!*' It was Jean. He was looking through a pair of binoculars.

As ever, the German's methodical necessity for promptness, meant that, as they had predicted, Dreschsler and his driver were climbing the hill towards the castle 20 minutes before they were due.

Jean, Yvette and George signalled with a nod of the head that they were ready.

George could feel his heart beating palpably.

221

Dreschsler entered the castle first, his luger in his hand at the ready. Following behind and also armed, was his driver. With silencers fitted, and suitably hidden from view, Jean levelled his gun at Dreschsler and George at his Dreschsler's driver. Jean looked anxiously at George. George nodded. Instantaneously, they pulled their triggers. Their aims were true and found their targets. Dreschsler and his driver were dead before they hit the ground. Yvette had her gun trained on both of them at the ready, just in case one of the shots missed their mark. Quickly Jean and George dragged the lifeless bodies to the shallow ditch. They stripped the driver and dressed him in Jean's spare clothing that they had brought with them. Carefully they poured petrol over them to create the desired effect as planned, and set them alight. Yvette stood by with a bucket filled with water that had been gathered up from a nearby spring. When just the desired cremation had occurred, the flames were doused. It was a hot day and the excess water would drain away quickly, soaked up by the dry earth. Leaving no trace of their deception. Yvette walked away to dispose of the bucket as George placed Jean's partially burned, false identity card into the scorched inside pocket of the driver's charred body. As he bent down, the smell was intense. He placed his hand over his mouth and nostrils. They both stood and looked at the scene making sure that it looked to be as they wished it to look. When a shot rang out. Both fell instinctively to the ground. George raised his gun, Jean had left his on the ground a little further away.

They looked desperately to see where the shot had originated.

'*Merde!*'

They looked at where the voice came from. It was Yvette. She was on the ground clutching her groin. Blood was oozing from a wound. Jean and George were confused. They couldn't see anyone else. Jean crawled over to Yvette.

'*I can't believe it Jean!*'

'What *happened* Yvette?' George was still sweeping the area with his gun.

Jean looked down and saw Dreschsler's luger next to her hand. He was confused.

'I picked it up and it just went off Jean. Oh *sweet Jesus!* What have I done.'

The Luger has a hair like trigger; a simple touch and it can discharge. She had picked it up to throw it into the ditch and it went off accidentally, the bullet passing into and through her groin.

George ran over.

'*Yvette!*'

He moved her hand away from the wound and tore at her trousers. The bullet had torn apart her

223

femoral artery. He looked up from the injury and into her eyes and she to him…and she knew.

'Yvette lie still. I will go for help,' said Jean. He looked at George. Out of sight of Yvette, George, with a melancholy expression, shook his head slowly.

Even though in great pain, she managed to be so brave. A stillness came over her.

'No Jean. I will not make it. I am done.' She looked at him and gave him a heartfelt smile. Then she looked at George, and passed to him the same sincere and profoundly warm smile.

'It's OK Jean. We have done what we came to do. We have completed our mission. My dearest and beautiful brother; continue the journey.'

Her eyes became cloudy, her pain lifted and a look of peace set across her face.

'*Yvette!*' Jean's tears traced the lines in his face and fell upon the dry earth. He knelt down and hugged her so tightly. George was moved to tears, also.

After a few moments, a woman's voice…

'What has *happened*?'

It was Sylvie.

'What are you *doing here* Sylvie?' asked George.

'I followed you and hid further down the hillside. She pulled out a gun. Just in case. I heard a shot. I knew that you had silencers and that something

224

must have gone wrong.' She looked at George then Jean; then she saw Yvette.

She let out a blood-curdling cry.

'*No! No no no*!' She knelt down beside her and held her in her arms. She rocked her gently as you would a baby to sleep.

After a short time, they had gathered their senses enough to know that they had to finish the task. The determination and necessity…was even more so now.

'I will take care of Yvette,' said Sylvie. 'You both have to leave.'

Jean was still reeling in disbelief of what had happened.

'I can't leave her here.'

'*Now Jean*! You must go *now*!'

Her exclamation shocked him enough for him to collect his thoughts, and focus on what had to be done next.

Sylvie repeated what she had said, 'I *will* take care of Yvette Jean. I promise you. She will not be left here. You must carry on as planned. Other people's lives depend on it. Do you understand?'

Jean nodded quiescently.

Their journey onwards to Spain continued with few words spoken between them.

The plan unfurled without any further difficulties or complications. They abandoned their car and continued on foot as prearranged. They met with their contact two kilometres from the border.

They crossed into Spain at 16:42.

CHAPTER TWENTY-FOUR

Monday 17th April 2023

Saint-Goustan

I looked at Pascal; we were both speechless. He, as I, was clearly astonished and surprised by what Pierre had just told us. I'm not sure how much Pascal knew, but on the face of it, it wasn't considerable.

I let out a deep sigh.

'Well. That's thrown up more questions than answers.'

Pascal nodded in an agreement.

'How much of that were you aware of Pascal?'

He shook his head slowly from side to side.

'Only parts of it. My father had told me some of it, but…I don't know, it was different somehow.'

I looked at Pierre.

'That's how it all works isn't it Pierre.' It was rhetorical.

227

He looked penetratingly at me.

'Yes. I'm afraid it is Alice. It has to be that way. As you have just heard, there are many deceptions and duplicities and sometimes there is a need to alter things a little.'

'You mean; my father didn't tell me the truth?' questioned Pascal.

'No. Your father told you the absolute truth. Only, it was the truth that *he* knew it to be.'

'You don't trust each other?'

'Yes we do. Of course we do. But it is safer sometimes to withhold or change something in order to mislead others that might threaten us.'

I asked him again.

'What is your organisation Pierre? I mean, what does it represent?'

He gave his answer some thought before continuing.

'We are bound by rigorous instructions. We cannot break secrecy, repeat information or reveal ethical codes. What we do, we see as *good* work. We are trying to make the World a safer and better place; one in which *all* humanity can live and thrive together. Sometimes, we come across other earlier, and occasionally from the very distant past, mysteries, secrets and riddles, that are unrelated directly to our work; but which could have an influence on what we do, if we didn't act.'

228

I couldn't know for sure; but I had an idea which organisation it might possibly be. I had previously taken an interest in their activities and undertakings; but I was unable to uncover anything of significance. He would of course never admit to it, but...

'Bilderberg?'

Pierre, clearly experienced in surreptitious deception, showed no emotion and gave nothing away. Pascal however, looked furtively to Pierre, and gave everything away.

'Hmm,' I muttered. 'You need to practice your facial reaction Pascal. It could get you into a lot of trouble.'

He gave me an impassive stare.

'Yeah. Better,' I said, with a wry grin.

Another silence fell momentarily before returning to more pertinent and more profound questions.

'The greeting Yvette and the reply George gave when they first met, "*Cognoscere hostem tuum. Non sum inimicus tuus.*" What does it mean? Is that to do with your organisation or group or whatever?'

Pierre smiled broadly.

'You have a good sense of recall Alice.'

'Yes. It's a handy attribute to have if you're a novelist.' I reiterated, 'Your group Pierre?'

229

'No.'

'No? Is that *it*?'

'The greeting is a sort of cryptogram.'

'Cryptogram?'

'A verbal code to recognise and confirm who you are.'

He looked at me as if willing me to figure it out. I thought briefly.

'Défenseur de la foi.'

'*Cognoscere hostem tuum* - know your enemy. *Non sum inimicus tuus* - I am not your enemy.'

'Very Dan Brown.'

He narrowed his eyes; then a realisation.

'Ahh yes. Another novelist.'

I grinned.

'I'm not in the same league.'

'You might be after all this,' added Pascal.

I turned and looked at him. He was sporting a schoolboy grin.

'Very good that Pascal,' I said nodding my head in a slightly patronising way. 'So, you're saying that my great grandfather was involved with the brotherhood of Défenseur de la foi?'

Pierre nodded.

'Did you know Pascal?'

He shook his head.

'No I didn't Alice.'

I believed him.

'Is my father Pierre?'

'I don't know the answer to that Alice.'

'Is my father connected in some way to your group?'

He shook his head.

'No.'

I took a few moments to chew it over…

'Do you know where Yvette is buried Pierre?'

'Yes. Sylvie did as she promised. Without any interference from the Germans, she and the villagers managed to arrange a funeral for her. She is buried in the church graveyard in Dio-et-Valquières. It is a beautiful and quiet place where she lies.'

'I think I would like to go there one day.'

'I think she would like that Alice,' he said with a nod of his head and a warm smile.

'It's more than a little strange that this happened where it all began; in Béziers.'

'Yes. History seemingly repeating itself.'

'It has to be more than coincidence,' I said. 'There must be a reason?' As he has yet to perfect the art of the indifferent, non-displaying, facial expression, I looked straight at Pascal. He clearly had no idea. I looked at Pierre.

'What do you think Pierre?'

In that very French way of being non-committal, he shrugged his shoulders and jutted out his chin.

'I don't know Alice. Maybe there is something in it. I simply don't know.'

Do I believe him?

'What was it that Jean was guarding? That people have died to keep secret. Was it knowledge, the whereabouts of an artefact, a manuscript?' Then it hit me. Why it hadn't occurred to me before as the story was unfolding I have *absolutely* no idea.

'Could it have been a letter?'

Bingo! That seemed to hit home.

Once again, Pierre and the look of the non-committal. But the look on Pascal's face said it all.

'Is it Pierre?' asked Pascal. 'Is that the reason my father was killed? *Is it*?'

Pierre looked apologetically at him.

'I don't know what Jean was keeping safe Pascal. And that's the truth. I think that whatever it was, or is, comes from a distant past. Maybe the *Défenseur de la foi* have been guarding a secret; maybe not. I, we, simply do not have any evidence. It is not our business.' He looked at me, 'not unlike you Alice, we have inadvertently been dragged into the situation. Are paths have now crossed. But it was not our concern.'

'It is now Pierre,' said Pascal. 'We have to find out where that letter is, and what it contains. I need to

232

know why my father was murdered. I thought it was something to do with our group. But it isn't; is it Pierre?'

He looked sympathetically at Pierre.

'I have been making enquires Pascal.'

'Do you know what happened to Jean after he reached Spain?' I asked.

He looked apprehensive.

'Yes.'

'What is it Pierre,' I quizzed.

'After the war we know that Jean returned to Dio-et-Valquières, clearly it was to see where his sister's last resting place was, and to pay his last respects to her. However, the day after his arrival, he vanished.'

Both Pascal and I were puzzled.

'Vanished?' I asked.

He nodded.

'Yes.'

'Do you think some harm came to him?'

'We don't know. He was last seen by the riverside. And then, nothing. He just vanished without trace.'

'That was the last time anyone saw him,' questioned Pascal?'

He nodded.

'Yes.'

It might just be me seeing connections where there may not be any, but I recalled the drowning of

Richard de Merclesden in a river. Another coincidence?

'This inheritance; this legacy, it just continues doesn't it Pierre,' I said.

He nodded.

'Yes. I'm afraid it seems it does Alice.'

He let out a sigh.

I continued, 'How did Dreschsler have knowledge about what it was that Jean had, or knew?'

'All I can tell you is what we *think* happened. Some of it we know as true, other, without evidence, is partly conjecture...putting two and two together as you English say. It is recorded that Dreschsler was instrumental in the torture of French Jews for the Ahnenerbe, that he was pursuing on the orders of Himmler. Himmler was convinced that the Jews had a greater knowledge of many historical manifestations and occurrences. We believe that as Dreschsler was interrogating a prisoner, he, as did we, inadvertently stumbled across something that he knew was of vital importance and of significance to the activities of the Ahnenerbe. Something ancient. How he made the connection to Jean, we may never know?'

'Did anyone come to search for Dreschsler?' asked Pascal.

'We do know that Dreschsler had a son, Karl, who was aged twenty-five at the time of Dreschsler's demise. He was an SS officer in the Wehrmacht. Again, it is our belief and presumption that Dreschsler had passed on that knowledge to his son previously. We do know that his son went to Dio-et-Valquières. He didn't make any enquires in the village, but he did go up to the castle. As with Jean, after the war, he simply disappeared. We did however; pick up his trail a little later on. We found a birth certificate for the birth of a boy; Franz Dreschsler born 15th July 1948, Frankfurt: Father, Karl Dreschsler, Father's occupation: Clerk to the shipping trade. That's what his father's occupation had been before the war. His whereabouts after 1948 and that of his son, are unknown.'

'Unknown?' I said.

He nodded.

'Yes.'

We sat there not for the first time in silence attempting to make some sort of sense out of the events that had, and are apparently still are occurring…

'I thought it time to lighten if possible, the conversation.

'If nothing else, one thing has clearly come out of this Pascal.'

'What?'

235

'The ease and predisposition in which my family seems able to jump into bed with the French.'

Smiles from both Pascal and Pierre was just what was needed. I looked at the kitchen wall clock. It was 12:47.

'I don't know about you two; but I'm hungry.'

'I'm so sorry Alice,' said Pascal apologetically. 'And to you too Pierre. I'll make us something to eat.'

I continued, 'It's such a nice day. Why don't we go to one of the harbour side cafés?'

They both nodded their approval. Pierre was a little more hesitant.

'Do you think it's safe Pierre?'

He smiled broadly but not reassuringly enough for my liking.

'We have to eat. Let's go.'

CHAPTER TWENTY-FIVE

Monday 17th April 2023
15:38
Saint-Goustan

We had eaten, and after a short walk we sat on a bench by the water's edge. The conversation turning once again to the current situation…

'I have to make arrangements with the Port authority to sail you back to the UK Alice,' said Pierre.

'Will I be safe do you think? I mean it's all a bit of a mess really, isn't it?'

'You are not in possession of the letter. It was clearly intended for you, but whosoever has it, has put you out of,' he hesitated, 'harm's way.'

'Danger you mean Pierre.'

He shrugged his shoulders.

'What I'm saying is, that there is no need for any contact with you now. You have nothing to offer them.'

'As far as you know?'

'That's what I believe.'

I let out a sigh. There was a part of me that wanted to know more; a conclusion to it all. However, there was another part of me that wished to prolong my longevity.

'Are you OK Alice?' asked Pascal.

I smiled.

'Yes. I'm fine Pascal.' He leaned into me and kissed me tenderly on the lips.

Pascal sat back into the bench.

'I still don't understand the connection to my father. How and why was he in possession of the letter, and whatever it contains?'

Pierre looked at him apologetically and clearly didn't have the answer.

'I didn't know about the letter Pascal. He told me nothing about that.'

Once again there was a considered pause...

'I have already got clearance to leave France tomorrow morning, but I need to give them the arrival point. Where would be the best place for me to sail you to?' asked Pierre.

I thought about it for a moment. Although I should return home, I wanted a little time to think things through before speaking to my family, and of course because he has helped me so much in this search, Noah. We have a house in Dartmouth that my grandfather Thomas bought years ago. I have so many happy memories there, both as a child and teenager, and, to be honest, that's what I needed right now…a little peace and quiet.

'We have a house in Dartmouth. I could do with a little tim…'

'*Dartmouth*?' Interjected Pierre, with an expression of bafflement and probing eyes.

I was equally puzzled by his reaction, as was Pascal. 'Yes. Is everything OK Pierre? If it's too out of the way?'

He shook his head.

'No no. Dartmouth is fine. It's just that…' he shook his head, '…it's no matter. I'll make the call.'

I sensed there was more to this story than was being told. And I had the distinct feeling that Dartmouth had a part to play in it.

Pierre stood. 'I'll make the call.' He walked over to the quayside. I was becoming suspicious of everything and I wondered why he couldn't have just contacted them about the return destination, here, sat on the bench? Then again, perhaps he simply just needed to stretch his legs. This slight

239

paranoia was fine for characters that I create in my books; but not for me in real life. Although, weirdly there was a part of me that was still enthralled and excited by it all, and that bothered me. The consequence of all that has happened is appalling and abhorrent. People have been betrayed, tortured and died because of this unknown affair. I should be sickened by it, not fascinated.

A reassuring arm came around my shoulder.

'Are you alright Alice?' asked Pascal in a low and kindly voice.

I smiled affectionately at him.

'I'm fine Pascal. Thank you.'

'It's all too much isn't it Alice.'

I looked at him. He has lost his father, suddenly, and in the most horrific circumstances, and may never know why. But, he's sat next to me on this bench, comforting me. Other than Chloe and my mum and dad, I don't think I have ever met a more caring and thoughtful human being.

Pierre walked slowly back to the bench.

'It's done.'

'Thank you Pierre.'

He smiled warmly.

His reaction to the name Dartmouth however, still played on my mind.

'There *is* more isn't there Pierre?'

240

'More?'

'Yes Pierre,' I said perceptively.

He looked at me and pondered briefly…

'There *is* another story. It concerns George's son; your grandfather, Thomas.'

'You know about my *grandfather,* also?'

'Yes I do Alice. He was a *very* interesting character.'

I couldn't really think straight.

'Is there anything you *don't* know about my family?'

He passed over my question and continued, 'I think I can fill in a little more detail about Thomas, than Benoît told you. Would you like to hear *that* story Alice?'

I nodded.

'Are you kidding me. Of *course* I would. Why would I not.'

CHAPTER TWENTY-SIX

12:27, Tuesday 20th April 1965
Shropshire, England

The phone rang out…

'Thomas.'
'Yes.'
'It's Bradley.'
'Hello Bradley. How are you?'
'I'm good thanks. And you?'
'Yes all good here.'
There was a slight pause…
'It's raining cats and dogs here.'
Thomas knew that was a code informing him that there was a problem.
'Perhaps you should go somewhere else where the sun is shining.'
Bradley laughed.
'Yes, I was just thinking that myself.'
'Anywhere in particular?'

'Well the sun always seems to shine in the Mendips.'

Thomas laughed.

'Well, best go then.'

'You know what Thomas. I might just do that.

Thomas knew where he had to go; not the Mendips, but Devon; more specifically, Dartmouth.

'So, best pack your case Bradley,' continued Thomas.

'I think I'll do just that.'

They both laughed.

'Is that all you called me for?' asked Thomas.

'You know I always come to you for advice.'

Once again Bradley laughed.

'Right then. Thanks for the kick up the pants.'

Once again they both laughed.

'Bye Bradley.'

The call ended.

Thomas walked upstairs, took a small suitcase down from the top of his wardrobe and placed it on the bed. He then began to place a few items of clothing and a few toiletries inside it, and closed it to.

Within an hour, he was in his car and on his way to Dartmouth…

CHAPTER TWENTY-SEVEN

19:40, Tuesday 20th April 1965
Dartmouth

On the river embankment, Thomas was sat on a bench overlooking the river Dart. All was peaceful and the river ran meditatively and tranquil.

'Hello Thomas.'

He turned and smiled.

'Hello Bradley.'

Bradley sat down next to him.

'Any unwanted bystanders?'

Thomas shook his head.

'No. I wasn't followed.'

Bradley nodded.

'It so nice here,' said Thomas.

'Yes. Well, who knows; one day you might be able to afford to live here.'

He laughed.

'Do you really think so?' replied Thomas nonchalantly.

'No. Not really.'

'So?'

'We need you to do a Black Bag job.'

A 'Black bag job' is code for a covert entry into buildings or dwellings in order to obtain information for intelligence operations.

'OK'

'I've left the details in a toilet cistern across the road. I've placed a small red star on the top of the toilet door.'

Thomas grimaced.

'Red star. Are you kidding?'

Bradley laughed and nodded his head enthusiastically.

'Yeah.'

Thomas shook his head.

'You worry me sometimes.'

Bradley let out a boisterous laugh

After a few seconds Bradley's expression became more serious, he continued, 'We should all be worried comrade.'

Although he didn't show it, a small shiver ran down Thomas's spine. Bradley stood, smiled, turned and without looking back, walked down the embankment towards the area known as the Boat float.

After retrieving an envelope from the toilet cistern, and removing the red star, he headed back to his B&B for the night.

CHAPTER TWENTY-EIGHT

08:15, Wednesday 21st April 1965
Dartmouth

In the dining room, the B&B owner placed Thomas's breakfast on the table in front of him and smiled convivially.

'Are you sure I can't tempt you to stay at least another day or two?' She asked impishly. 'It's a beautiful place, lots to see and explore.'

Thomas smiled.

'I have to be someplace else I'm afraid.'

'Oh, I see,' she replied, with a playful grin. 'Someplace else eh. That sounds mysterious and interesting.'

Thomas smiled, nodded and thought to himself, "if only she knew just how near to the mark she was."

'It is beautiful here though. I'll definitely be coming back.'

She gave a broad smile.

'Well, there you are then. Enjoy your breakfast.'
Thomas smiled, buttered a slice of toast and sat back into his chair.

With the bill duly settled, he placed his case into the boot of his car, and set off for Shropshire…

CHAPTER TWENTY-NINE

15:47, Wednesday 21st April 1965
Shropshire.

Thomas's phone rang out…

'Hello.'

'Thomas. It's Charles.'

Charles is Thomas's handler in MI5

'Hello Charles.'

'How was your appointment?'

Appointment meant rendezvous with Bradley. They were never absolutely certain that their conversations weren't being listened in to.

'The appointment went well. I have a new Job Charles. One that might further my career.'

Furthering his career was an assignment abroad.

He looked down at the contents of the envelope that he had opened earlier.

'I start my training tomorrow.'

'That's good news. Tomorrow though? Don't you have a dentist appointment tomorrow?'

'Oh yes. I'd forgotten.'

'I'd let them know today and try and reschedule.'

Let them know and reschedule, meant he was to arrange any equipment and papers needed with his office in MI5.

'I will. Thanks Charles. I don't know where I would be without you.'

'Actually, I'm passing your dentist in a short while. I'll get you a new appointment. I'll tell them that you're feeling under the weather.'

Feeling under the weather meant that Charles wanted to meet with him urgently.

'Thanks Charles. That'll save a little time.'

'I have to take my car into the garage, so it fits in with me.'

The garage was code for the meeting place. The small church at Wem Park and Gardens.

'OK. Thanks again Charles.'

'Good luck with the new Job.'

'Thanks. I hope that your car doesn't cost you the earth.'

Cost the earth, was the time...midday.

'Yes. Indeed. Speak soon Thomas.'

'Bye Charles. Thanks again.'

Thomas arrived at the church at 11:54. A voice came from behind him.

'Hello Thomas.'

He turned to see a cheery faced Charles.

'Hello Charles.'

'Let's walk,' suggested Charles.

'So, what's the brief?'

'It's a Black bag job.'

He nodded.

'I see. Where?'

'Acasta, Berlin.'

Charles narrowed his eyes.

'Acasta?'

'Yes. Do you know of it?'

'Yes I do.' He seemed a little uneasy.

'Charles?'

'Acasta is where records of high ranking German officers' statements, reports and testimonies from the Second World War are held. Not just any old Germans. But…'

'What is it?'

'You have to be very careful with this assignment Thomas. You will need to keep your wits about you. Don't trust anyone.'

Thomas laughed.

'You are kidding Charles.' Meaning that his job as an agent in MI5 was riddled with intelligence, deceptions, duplicities, treachery, informers and counter espionage. 'Don't trust anyone?'

Charles stopped walking and held his arm. He looked anxious.

'*No one*! Do you understand Thomas?'

Thomas was a little taken aback. He had never seen Charles exhibit agitation and unease before he was always so calm and collected.

Thomas nodded.

'I will Charles. I promise you,' he said, reassuringly.

'What is it they want specifically?'

'They want the records that are kept in Department 2, Section 27.'

Charles looked down to the ground.

'Anything else?'

'No. I've got clearance as an IT engineer. A pass will be waiting for me at the Reception desk.'

Charles nodded.

'OK. You get it…and get out as quickly as you can. Then back home.'

'It's all sorted. I've booked the flights and a hotel for the night.'

'Contact me the moment you land.'

He nodded.

'I will Charles.'

Charles put out his hand; Thomas reciprocated.

They shook and went their own separate ways.

Charles's uneasiness had affected Thomas a little. Charles clearly knew more than he was letting on. But absence of information, was the business sometimes, he knew that. Operatives were only told what they needed to know. Sometimes for their own safety. His father George had told him as much, after Thomas had been recruited into MI5 from Cambridge University on the strength of his father's involvement with the SOE. His father had shared many things about subservience and wariness and what it takes to belong to, and work inside, a clandestine and surreptitious organisation.

At home he prepared everything for the following day. Unusually for him, as he was always focused; his sleep was disrupted by unease and hesitation…

CHAPTER THIRTY

11:28, Thursday 22nd April 1965
Berlin.

After exiting through the airport's revolving doors a man stepped forward.

'Thomas?'

'Yes.'

'I'm John; a friend of Bradley's.'

Thomas shook his hand.

John took Thomas's small suitcase from him.

'This way please.'

John had a very strong Mid-Western American accent. He walked over to a car and opened the door for Thomas. He then placed Thomas's suitcase on the back seat. John got in, closed the door behind him, and proceeded to drive off.

A little further on, and John broke the silence.

'Everything you need is in the boot. I'll drop you off at Acasta, and then pick up at your hotel tomorrow morning and drive you back to the airport. Your flight is at: 07:10. Is that right?'

Thomas nodded.

'Yes.'

'I'll be there at 05:00. After Acasta; I'll go to your hotel and drop off your suitcase at the Reception desk.'

Once again Thomas gave a nod of the head.

'That's fine.'

Whilst John was still driving, with one hand he reached into the glove compartment and pulled out a personal name card. He passed it to Thomas.

'Just in case anything goes wrong. Call me.'

'OK.'

Thomas slipped the card into his inside pocket. What he hadn't told John or Charles however, was that he had changed his return flight to the UK. He had booked his return flight at 18:45. Mindful of Charles's warning, "don't trust anyone" he thought it prudent to get out of Berlin ASAP. As he couldn't be certain that his movements weren't being observed; after getting the information from Acasta, he would have to go to the hotel to pick up his suitcase. He would check in and pay there and then at the Reception. He would freshen up before leaving through a side tradesman's entrance; then a taxi to the airport, and home.

John pulled up outside Acasta. There was no name on the building, just a number. Thomas got out, walked around to the boot, lifted out a small bag of tools, shut the boot and leaned in through the open passenger window.

'See you tomorrow John.'

John smiled and nodded.

'You betcha.'

He drove off.

Thomas walked into the building and over to the Receptionist. She gave him a pleasing easy smile.

'Hello. How may I help you?'

'My name is Peter Johnson.' He took out an ID badge and showed it to her. 'I've been asked to look at one of your machines, in Department 2 section...'

He took out a job invoice from his tool bag.

'27,' she said with another smile.

He nodded and smiled.

'Yes.'

She gave him a building pass and a code for the door.

'Take the lift to the 2nd floor, turn left, down the corridor and it's on your right.'

He nodded.

'Thank you.'

'You're welcome.'

Once inside the room, he found the draw labelled Section 27. He opened the draw and took out the file. He then removed a small camera from his inside pocket. Without reading what it contained he began to photograph each page. He used up his film and had to replace it with another. He continued until he reached the last page. Swiftly, he replaced the file and closed the draw. He left the room and walked down the stairwell to the Reception.

'That was quick,' she said, with an easy effervescent smile.

He reached into his bag and pulled out an electrical switch. He held it up to show her.

'Easy work today. I'll book it down as a two hours Job.' He winked. 'I've got myself a little time for a coffee.'

She grinned.

'Your secret's safe with me.' He thought about the irony of her sentiment.

He passed her the building pass.

'Bye then.'

She smiled.

'Bye Peter.' He turned and looked at her...she winked at him. He left the building and walked a little way down the road before turning down an alleyway. In front of him were a couple of large commercial waste containers. He looked furtively around him. He opened up one of the lids and after removing his bogus job sheet, threw the tool bag into the bin. He walked back to the road and hailed a taxi to take him to the hotel.

Having checked in, paid, and picked up his suitcase, he made his way to his room. He took out the job sheet, tore it up into small pieces and flushed it down the toilet. He looked at his watch: 13:42. He had just enough time for a quick shower. He would get something to eat when at the airport.

He had finished his shower, dried himself and stepped back into his room, when a hand was placed over his mouth. He struggled but within moments, he was unconscious…

CHAPTER THIRTY-ONE

Time, unknown, date unknown,
whereabouts…unknown

Slowly he opened his eyes. A male voice…

'It's OK. Take your time.'

He looked up. The voice came from a man with an American accent, roughly in his mid-thirties whom was sat on a chair opposite to him.

'How are you feeling Thomas?'

Lying on a mattress on the floor, he was feeling drowsy and utterly confused.

'Where am I? And who are you?'

'That's not really important right now.'

Who ever the man was, he clearly knew who, *he* was.

'It's important to me.'

'Well…that's life isn't it.'

Thomas sat up on the mattress.

The man stood, walked over to a wooden cabinet, picked up a jug of water and poured out some of its contents into a glass. He walked over to Thomas and offered it to him. Thomas eyed it suspiciously.

'Do you think we would poison you before we have had chance for a chat? Really? Drink it. It will help.'

Thomas took the glass and took a sip. It did taste refreshing. He placed the glass on the floor next to him.

'Chloroform?'

The man nodded.

'It's quick acting and easy to administer. It seems to do the trick.'

'Can't disagree with that.'

The man gave him a smile.

'Let's keep it simple. Where's the film Thomas?'

'Film?'

The man let out a sigh.

'Photographs. We have the camera but not the film, or films.'

Thomas shrugged his shoulders.

'I don't know what you're talking about? Who are you?'

'We know that you are a Communist spy Thomas.'

Thomas's blood ran cold.

'Do you know we can lock you up, and throw away the key. No one would ever know.'

Thomas stared at him dispassionately.

'Who are you?'

Picking up on his American accent…

'CIA?'

The man's expression was equally non-committal.

'Why were you taking photographs of details of American Military personnel?'

Thomas didn't know if what he was saying was a ruse.

'I don't know what you're talking about. I'm an IT engineer and I went to fix an electrical switch that had malfunctioned.'

The man let out another sigh.

'Where are your tools? Where is the switch? Where is the Job memorandum confirming any of what you say?' He sat back into his chair. 'Take your time,' he said calmly.

He thought about it momentarily. If he told him that he had disposed of the tools and switch into the waste container, it would only raise more questions and suspicions. Thomas knew he was in deep trouble.

'You are a Communist spy aren't you Thomas?'

He shook his head. Whoever he was, it was clear he had enough information for him to be certain that Thomas was a Communist spy.

'Hungry?' The man said with a cheery smile.

Thomas nodded his head.

'Yes actually. I am.'

The man smiled again.

'I'll get you something.'

He stood walked over to a door, knocked and turned back to Thomas.

'Clever move that.'

'What was clever?'

'Changing your flight. Smart.'

The door opened, he stepped out of the room and the door was closed behind him.

He got up from the mattress and sat down on another chair by a table. He looked around him; it was a windowless room, so he didn't know whether is was day or night; and there were no objects or artefacts in the room to give any indication as to where he was. His watch was missing from his wrist, so he had no idea of the time. He knew they were letting him stew…

After about 20 minutes, give or take, the door opened and the man walked into the room carrying a tray with food on it. He placed it in front of Thomas and smiled.

'Enjoy. I'll be back later, and we can have another little chat.'

He left the room leaving Thomas once again alone with his thoughts…

A further period of unknown duration elapsed, when once again, the door opened and the man entered.

'Finished?' He asked smiling.

Thomas nodded. The man continued, 'That's OK. No need to thank me.'

'You know my name. Could you tell me yours?'

He nodded.

'Of course; it's Henry. Whether you believe me or not, well…that's all a part of the game, isn't it?'

'Well at least I can call you something. I'm intrigued Henry. How did you get me…here?'

He sat thoughtfully for a moment.

'I think it's OK to tell you that. We got ourselves an ambulance and uniforms and told the nice lady on Reception that you had made a call to say that you were feeling unwell.' He stopped and smiled. 'You get the picture don't you Thomas.'

'Very clever. You just carried me out on a stretcher.'

'Yes we are rather good at this stuff.'

'CIA?'

'Well…you see it's a choice thing isn't it. CIA, MI5, KGB, the Stasi? So much choice. We know who you are though Thomas.' He reached inside his pocket. He placed a card on the table. Thomas picked it up it was the card that the driver that had picked him up from the airport had given to him.

'John Singer. Is a known, well, known to *us* at least, Communist spy. Your friend, Bradley, is a known Communist spy. Really Thomas; the company you keep.'

It was a huge gamble, but Thomas was now convinced that they *were* CIA. They could of course be anybody. They could even be acting on their own. The information that Thomas may have photographed could be worth a great deal of money and be very useful to certain people. However; it was his only choice.

'I'm with MI5. I have been acting as a double agent to infiltrate a Communist cell.'

Henry gave him a doubting smile.

'Hmm. No. I don't think so.'

'I am. And that's the truth.'

'Ahh. Truth, lies, falsehoods and fabrications. It's all part of it. It's hard to tell the truth from the untruth. It can get so confusing, that sometimes you get all muddled and begin to doubt yourself.'

'If you are who I think you are, then it should be easy for you to check me out.'

He sighed.

'OK Thomas. Let's just for the moment run with that and believe what you are saying is true. Who is your Handler?'

Thomas sat back into his chair.

'If I am who I say I am; you know that I can't give you that information.'

'Then where is your proof?'

'You have the capability and the means to check. I *know* you do.'

'Hmm. Possibly. Where are the films Thomas?'

As Thomas sat in his chair, suddenly he felt a sense of foreboding. He could feel it all going wrong. If he gave them the films, they, whomever they were, could just dispose of him. Whilst he alone had the knowledge of where the films were located…he was safe.

'OK Thomas. I can see that this is a little difficult for you. I'm going to leave you to think about your situation. I'll be back later to chat some more.'

He stood, knocked on the door and left the room.

The door opening awoke Thomas. He was lying once again on the mattress. He had no idea how long he had been sleeping.

Henry entered the room carrying a steaming hot mug of coffee. He placed it on the table.

'For you. A good strong coffee. Just what you need, I bet?'

Henry stared at Thomas with a blasé expression.

Thomas picked up the mug. He allowed him time to finish his coffee.

'We are going to move you now. You have a choice. Just like in the movies. We can do it the hard way or the easy way.' He removed a syringe from his jacket pocket...

Thomas awoke. He was in what seemed to be, a prison cell. There was a small window high up to allow in the light, but unreachable to be able to see out of. There was a toilet and washbasin in the corner. There was also soap, a flannel, a towel, toothbrush and toothpaste. He could not see or hear any other captives. He sat down on the single wooden chair. As he looked around him; a sickening realisation struck home. It was an isolation cell. He was totally, and utterly on his own...

CHAPTER THIRTY-TWO

Monday 17th April 2023
16:54
Saint-Goustan

Not for the first time, both Pascal and I were speechless. I took a few moments to absorb what Pierre had just told us.

'What happened to Thomas?' I asked.

'He spent the next two years in total isolation. Other than food, drink and change of clothing. Even then, when the guards came they refused to enter into any dialogue with him. He asked questions but he was ignored. The only one concession they made was to give him books to read. He was allowed to choose them. Although, even then, they wouldn't speak to him; he had to write his choice of books down.'

'Two years in isolation. *Oh my god*! That's inhuman.' I said, in absolute disbelief.

'*Why* Pierre?' asked Pascal.

Pierre shook his head.

'We don't know?'

I continued, 'my dad has never talked about *any* of this. *Why*? Why has he not mentioned this? It was his father for Christ sake. I don't understand?'

'I don't know for certain; but maybe he didn't tell your father. Maybe he has no idea what had taken place?'

'No. I can't *believe* that? He must have talked to his son about that?'

Then I thought about everything that has happened. The deceptions, the untruths, the ambiguous information, misleading and misinforming. Twisting and turning throughout my family's history. It has changed my life. Yet again, Benoît's statement rang so true, "You are not who you think yourself to be Alice".

Pierre continued, 'the very essence of espionage is secrecy and deception. Even Benoît got some of it wrong. He too was misinformed. Whether purposely or how do you say; lost in translation.'

'He spoke to no one in two years. I cannot begin to *imagine* how that would affect you in later life,' I said.

'It is probably the reason why he bought the house in Dartmouth. It seemed to be a happy place for him. A place he could find peace.'

Even though it was so long ago; I couldn't help tears running down my face. Then I looked at Pascal. After all *he* has been through, how could I be so self-seeking. He put his arm around me.

'It's OK Alice. It is understandable.'

I have never been so close to a boyfriend or partner to say the words, "I love you" than right now at this moment in time. I don't why, but I held back; I have always done so, and it's something I should work on to change.

'Why didn't MI5 do something?' asked Pascal.

Pierre shrugged his shoulders.

'It is possible that they didn't know where he was or what had happened to him. It wasn't an unusual occurrence for an agent, to just disappear during the Cold War. Either through defection, accidental death, or murder. Sometimes, it could be that they wanted to just melt away and lie low for a while. It was, and still is, an extremely hazardous and precarious business.'

'What actually happened to him? Did he escape or...'

'No. Apparently, one day, and without any forewarning; he was just released. He was taken to the airport and put on a flight for England.'

'Where had he been held?' I asked.

'It was an American military base in Wiesbaden in West Germany.'

'My grandfather was right then.'

'What do you mean Alice?' questioned Pascal.

'It was the CIA. It must have been.'

Pierre nodded.

'I can't see any reason to suspect it was anyone else.'

'But *why* Pierre. Why was he kept there? Was he a threat? They *clearly* knew he wasn't a Communist spy. They *must* have known that. Through intelligence and the good relationship and networking between America and the UK.'

'At the time Alice; there was a lot of mistrust and paranoia between the US and the UK. Information was not always shared readily.'

'Were the films ever recovered?' I asked.

He shook his head.

'I don't know what happened to the photographs.'

'Did he make contact with MI5 after his release?'

'Yes. They actually looked after him quite well…financially that is. His handler however, Charles Wexler, had vanished.'

Then a sudden and sickening realisation, that was so unexpected that my blood drained from me and my chest tightened so much, that I struggled to catch my breath.

'*Shit! No no no.*'

Pascal stood up and held me.

'*Alice.* What *is it*? Are you alright?'

A passing young couple were clearly perturbed.

'Alice?' said Pierre voicing his own concern.

'Noah.'

'Noah?' quizzed Pierre.

'Noah's family name…is Wexler.'

Both Pierre and Pascal were mystified and confused.

'I don't understand?' said Pascal.

'Just wait a minute. Wait. Let me think about this,' said Pierre, thoughtfully.

We sat there in total silence trying to see if, and where there was a connection. Then…

'Charles,' said Pierre.

'Charles what?' I asked.

'The German name for Charles, is Karl.'

'Karl?' queried Pascal.

I understood exactly his train of thought.

'Karl Dreschsler?'

Pierre nodded.

'It is just possible Alice.'

'What are you talking about?' asked Pascal.

Pierre continued, 'A translated derivative of Dreschsler; is Wexler.'

'You're saying that Karl Dreschsler and Charles Wexler are one and the same?' questioned Pascal.

'That's *exactly* what we are saying Pascal,' I said.

I leaned forwards and held my head in my hands.

'But who is Noah?' he asked.

'Karl or Charles, had a son, Franz. The reason we couldn't trace him is that he changed his name to Wexler. I'm guessing that then Franz later had a son: and that son...is Noah.' Pierre looked at me apologetically. 'I'm so sorry Alice. This whole thing has been a torment for you.' He looked at Pascal, 'and for you too Pascal. Neither of you deserve this.'

I let out a sigh.

'Where does this stop? *Bastard!* Noah you *utter bastard*! He's my sister's partner for Christ's sake.'

'What are you going to do Alice?' asked Pascal.

'I don't know. I need time to think. I have the advantage...at least I *think* I do. He doesn't know that I know. I'll stay in Dartmouth for a couple of days. I'll phone Chloe now and tell her that I will be staying here for a little while longer. I don't want anyone to know that I am back in the UK.'

'I'll come with you Alice,' said Pascal.

I shook my head and smiled.

'You dear kind man. No Pascal. This part of the puzzle is something that I have to sort out myself.

As Benoît, and *you* said Pierre; this is about tying up loose ends.'

Pascal nodded his head in agreement.

'I do have things to do here regarding my father.' He looked at me with a deeply warm expression. 'If you need me...I *will* come.'

I smiled wholeheartedly.

'I know Pascal. I know.'

'I can alert...'

'*No Pierre*! *No one* must know. Remember what Thomas's most trusted friend Charles said to him before he betrayed him, "don't trust anyone". He trusted him, and was deceived. I know he did it. And I know why. It was about revenge and retaliation for his father, Werner Dreschsler's death in Dio, at the castle. He wanted my grandfather to suffer for what had happened to his father. He could have planned anything for Thomas: had him killed and blamed the Communists, had him disappeared, blamed the CIA, say he had committed suicide.' I shook my head. 'No. He wanted him exactly where he knew he would suffer a callously slow, and mentally agonising obliteration. He ground him to dust.'

I took out my phone and tapped the number.

'Hi Chloe.'

response...

'Yes I'm good thanks. Loving Paris.'

273

response…

I laughed. 'How are things?'

response…

'That's great. How's mum and dad?'

response…

'And Noah?'

response…

I narrowed my eyes and looked at Pierre and Pascal. 'When?'

response…

'Where?' Pascal and Pierre began to suspect something was not right.

response…

I struggled to keep my voice from wavering.

'He didn't say anything to me about that?'

response…

'OK. I'm phoning to let you know that I'll be staying a bit longer.'

response…

I laughed. 'I know I know. A couple of days.'

'OK Chloe. Catch-you soon.'

response…

'Yes. You too. Bye.'

I held my phone and stared distressingly into the river.

'Alice. Are you alright Alice,' asked a concerned Pascal.

'Noah is here in France.'

Pierre and Pascal were both perplexed.

'He left for France the day before I arrived here.'

'Where is he Alice? Asked Pierre, expressively.

I shook my head.

'Chloe said that he had to visit a couple of places related to his University research work in Medieval studies. She said that he only found out the day before he left the UK for France.'

Pierre and Pascal sat in a quiet focused silence. They knew *exactly* what conclusion I had come to, and what I was thinking. I looked at Pascal remorsefully.

'I am so sorry Pascal.'

'It is not your fault Alice.'

'It could have been me who led him to your father?'

'No Alice. You are innocent of any misgivings. How can you know such things? It is not possible.'

A contemplative few moments followed. There was nothing more to say about it…

'We will leave early Alice,' said Pierre.

I nodded.

'Thank you Pierre.'

'You will have to take *great* care Alice,' he said, meaningfully.

'I know. I will Pierre.'

We had our meal, and then turned in for the night. Both Pascal and myself had no inclination for sex. We simply held each other tenderly and fell into sleep…

CHAPTER THIRTY-THREE

Tuesday 18th April 2023
07:30
Leaving Saint-Goustan

Throughout the sail back to England, I sat on deck going over and over and over, everything; contemplating and dissecting each piece of the puzzle. One thought that was *so* abhorrent to me that I couldn't dwell on it, was that it now seemed Noah was implicated in some way to Benoît's death and I had led Noah to him. Regardless of what Pascal had said to me, I could never forgive myself. I thought about the family tree information and how he had manipulated the material and how he must have used what he'd found for his own advantage. So much was spiralling through my mind. Whatever I was going to do next; had to be planned and decisive…

CHAPTER THIRTY-FOUR

Wednesday 19th April 2023
08:52
Dartmouth, England

I offered Pierre a bed for the night, but he had insisted that he slept on his motor yacht. He had set sail just after dawn.

I closed my door behind me, and began my walk down Newcomen Road. On my right was, I guess, the reason my grandfather Thomas fell in love with and bought a house here. It is *so* beautiful: the river Dart serenely wending its way to the Dart estuary. I stopped for a moment to watch the unique Kingswear/Dartmouth car ferry just leaving Bayards cove, using its powerful and distinctive little tug boat as it pivots around the ferry by use of a rope before lining up, tying off and heading towards Kingswear. Its movement is mesmerising; balletic even.

I continued my walk and dropped down onto the slope leading to The Dartmouth Arms and Bayards Cove Inn. I had come for breakfast, but took a few moments to sit on a bench on the quayside. It is so tranquil at this time of the morning. I imagined Thomas sitting here watching the ferry arriving and departing; the boats bobbing gently on the skin like surface of the river. It was so peaceful; it would have been a world away from his nightmare, and now mine as it had turned out. No comparison of course, but you catch my drift. I stood and walked down Lower Street to Café Alf resco. And yes, it is Alf resco. I quite easily found a table and chair Alfresco at Alf fresco...sorry I couldn't resist.

As I had eaten here before; I knew what I was having.

'Good morning.'

Stood at the side of me was a cheery young girl probably in her early twenties.

'Good morning.'

'What can I get you?'

'Could I have scrambled egg on brown toast please?'

'Sure no problem. Would you like a drink?'

'I'd like a fresh orange; I'll take that now, and a coffee with the breakfast.'

'Perfect. It that everything?'

I nodded and smiled.

'Yes thank you.'

'Thank you.' With a smart turn and a swish of her French plait she walked back inside the café.

The ferry had just pulled up the slipway; disgorged its cars and a few foot passengers. Lower Street is a one-way street, and you know when the ferry has docked. A steady stream of vehicles...then the short quiet time before the next ferry.

'Your orange juice.' She placed it on the table, turned, and proceeded to clear a table as the only other people in the café, a young couple, had just left.

After about 10 minutes…
'Your breakfast.'
'Thank you.'
'Would you like any dressing with your breakfast?'
I smiled.
'No thank you. This is just fine.'
She turned and left.
I sprinkled over a little course ground black pepper; and it was good to go. The eggs were delightful; organic and sourced locally. There are so many farms in and around Dartmouth that quite a lot of the restaurants and cafés use locally sourced produce, which makes the meal so much more flavoursome and delicious.

As the weather seemed to be set fair for the day, I walked down to the Embankment. As I arrived, the red and cream Dittisham - or Ditsum as it is known locally, ferry docked at the pontoon. It is a small ferry that, depending on its cargo, can hold about 12 passengers. It takes a half hour to sail to Dittisham. A couple with an energetic young Springer Spaniel called Bess - that wasn't a guess, the owner called her name - alighted and walked up the pontoon steps. I stood at the top of the steps and called out to the skipper.

'Room for one?'

'Absolutely,' came the response from a young smiley chap. I love the idea of spontaneity. I walked out of the house this morning for breakfast and now I'm on my way to Ditsum. I walked down the steps and on to the boat.

'What time would you like to return?'

'2pm?'

'That's fine. I'll book you in.'

I paid him and sat myself down at the stern.

As we pulled away from the pontoon, I was the only passenger on board.

The reassuring, constant drone and pitch of the boat's engine was hypnotic. As the main course of the river widened out at Old Mill Creek, on the left we passed by the prettily located Kiln Gate Cottage; secluded, and serenely peaceful. From this point the river narrowed slightly. To the left and right the banks and steep hillsides are draped in ancient woodland, their canopies reaching dramatically skywards and whose roots are gnarled and snake along the woodland floor and then down to the high tide watermark where they hung in mid-air awaiting a rising tide and sweet water. On a mudflat, a young cormorant perched motionless on a fossilised tree trunk; its wings outstretched, drying in the sunshine as a heron flew overhead; slowly and gracefully flapping its wings rhythmically as it delineated the meandering course of the river as if guiding the way. With a "glug" a fish surfaced fleetingly, but as quickly as it had appeared it was gone. On the river's skin, a few small bubbles and placid ripples left their signature. All life seemed to be in a symbiosis. The whole picture was one of serenity; a oneness with nature. The sounds, the scents, the visual sequence, the tranquillity; it was utterly delightful.

As we sailed into a meander the other Dartmouth/Dittisham ferry, the Sandpiper, was approaching. The skipper raised his hand, which in turn was acknowledged by my skipper. I couldn't think of anything I would rather be doing, or anywhere I would rather be right now, other than this little piece of paradise.

On our left, or port side if you want to get nautical, we glided by the Anchor Stone, Greenway and Mill pool lay off to our right…starboard. Dittisham was in sight.

We pulled alongside the pontoon and I got off the boat.

'Thank you. That was lovely.'

He beamed an easy smile.

'You're welcome.'

'Do you ever get complacent about all this?'

His smile returned and he shook his head.

'No.'

'You are a very luck man.'

'I know,' he said, confidently.

'See you at two.'

'Enjoy your visit.'

I smiled, nodded and gave him a small wave and set off walking down the pontoon. As I walked towards the Ferry Boat Inn, memories came flooding back of crabbing excitedly from the pontoon as a child with Chloe, as my mum and dad, sat upon the quayside wall, watching us, usually with a glass of something in hand.

I walked off the end of the small bridge that connects the pontoon to the road. I passed by the Ferry Boat Inn and continued to walk up the road a short distance until I came to a lane going off to the right. It is appropriately named…The Lane.

A meander down The Lane is a must if visiting Ditsum. It is the very embodiment of an ageless

English lane; with ancient hedgerows, a scattering of thatched cottages and beautiful views.

I followed the lane until it ended at a path. A turn to the right and a small fresh water stream that trickles, trips and tumbles its way to the river, ran alongside. The path brought me to a large open space, where there is a small children's park and play area. The rest of the space is given over to the view. It is, for want of a simple superlative, gorgeous. I sat down on a bench and looked across the river. It is, I believe, at its widest point here. A calmness and serenity came over me. I was so glad I made the decision to come to Dartmouth rather than going home to Knutsford with all the baggage I would have carried with me. This will give me an opportunity for a little thought and composure.

I went over everything that had happened since taking my book to Shakespeare and Company, Paris; to arriving at this bench today.

A seagull landed noisily by the bench which shocked me back into the here and now. I had lost track of time and I had a ferry booked for 2pm. I looked at my phone: 12:23. I had plenty of time. Sitting here, cleansed me. I knew what I had to do next regarding the events of the past few months.

I took the decision to go home tomorrow. I was ready to face what lay ahead.

I booked tickets for the train from Paignton to Manchester, Piccadilly, and then another from Piccadilly to Knutsford. That all done, I set off for the ferry to take me back to Dartmouth.

As the river was at low ebb, I was able to take a shortcut along a gravel path and under a private pier back to the Ferry Boat Inn, where I sat on the wall watching the few children that were crabbing, as I waited for the ferry to come into view.

In the evening, I had a fish and chips take-away from, The Wheelhouse. The fish was just divine and cooked to perfection. I sat and ate it on the embankment. I promised myself that I would come back for a longer stay…very soon.

I walked back to the house and packed my case. What lay ahead was going to be a bumpy and difficult few days; especially for Chloe. That relationship had to come to an end. She would be utterly devastated and confused, as she really cares for Noah. Strange, or maybe not so strange, but when his name came into my head, I was filled with such a rage. I would have to temper that, and take a calm control of what I was about to say, and do…

CHAPTER THIRTY-FIVE

Thursday 20th April 2023
09:47
Paignton railway station

The train pulled in on time. As it was a direct train, I had been a little extravagant and booked 1st class. The journey takes about 5 hours, and one that I was looking forward to; especially the first part of the journey that delineates river and sea and passes through Dawlish and Teignmouth. I have wanted to travel this journey by train for such a long time, and now had the opportunity to do so.

The journey passed without delays and I arrived at Piccadilly pretty much on time at 15:07. My connection to Knutsford was on a different platform, platform 8, and was due to leave at 16:10. I walked down the platform and went into one of the station cafés.

I ordered a coffee and a cheese and ham baguette. It was nice enough, but not the same quality as my baguette from the supermarket back in France, and the backdrop was less intriguing!

My train was on time and I arrived in Knutsford at 16:51. I took a taxi for home.

I put my key in the lock, turned it, and entered my home. I placed my case on the hallway floor.

'Hello darling.' It was my mother.

'Hello mum.'

'Chloe said you would be arriving back tomorrow?'

'I decided to come back a day earlier. I'm itching to pick up where I left off with my book.'

She gave me a hug.

'Hello Alice.' It was my dad.

He beamed a smile, walked over to me and hugged me. Usually when he hugged me, and I him, it was of love and warmth; I felt so many emotions as he held me this time, knowing what I now know about his family history. It had altered things.

'How was your trip?'

I thought about a little descriptive licence.

'I *loved* Paris. *So* much going on and *so* much history.'

He smiled.

'Is Chloe around?'

'She's off shift at seven o'clock.'

My mum continued, 'I don't know if you knew; but by coincidence, Noah was in France whilst you were there Alice.'

I nodded.

'Yes. Chloe told me.' I managed a forced faux smile. 'What are the chances?'

'Did he contact you? asked my dad.

I shook my head.

'No. I guess he was busy. France is a big place. The chances of being in the same town or village at the the same time is…slim.' I don't know how I kept myself so calm and focused.

'Would you like something to eat?' asked my mum.

'No thanks. I'm good for now. I grabbed something at Piccadilly whilst I was waiting for my connection.'

'You did well with the trains Alice,' said my dad.

'How do you mean?'

'There are strikes all over the network at the moment.'

I nodded.

'Oh yes. I did see a notice at the station about strike days. I was lucky I guess.'

'How was the Paignton to Piccadilly journey.' Asked my dad. 'I know you've wanted to do that since you were a teenager.'

I smiled.

'It was fabulous. I'm *definitely* going to do that again one day.'

'Did you manage to get a window seat, to take in the views?'

I gave him and impish grin.

'First Class. *Big* window.'

He gave a small laugh.

'There's no other way to travel.'

'Coffee?' asked my mum.

'Coffee would be good. I'll just take my case upstairs.'

'OK. Bring any washing down with you and I'll do it now for you.'

'You do the coffee mum and I'll do my washing.'

She smiled.

'OK darling.'

I walked up the stairs and placed my case on top of my bed. I looked around the room and uncontrollably I began to cry. Although it took me by surprise, it's not unexpected I guess. The human mind copes with difficult situations, habitually with instinct without allowing too many emotions to get in the way of the process. But afterwards, there has to be a healing.

After unpacking, I walked back down the stairs and into the kitchen.

'Your coffee is in the conservatory,' said my mum.

291

'Thanks mum.'

I placed my laundry into the washing machine, started the cycle, and followed behind my mum.

I sat down on the sofa, picked up my coffee and took a sip.

'That's so good. Hit the spot.'

'So. Tell us all about Paris,' asked my dad.

Back in Dartmouth I had worked everything out: the order and information that I was going to tell them.

'There is quite a lot to tell you. If it's OK with you though, could it wait until Chloe gets home and I can tell you all together?'

They both nodded

'Of course darling. It makes sense.'

I looked at my dad. He had a distant and reflective look on his face. I couldn't know for sure of course; but he looked a little apprehensive.

'Are you OK dad?'

'Pardon?'

'You seem a little...distant.'

'What? No not at all. I was just thinking about...Oh I don't know, I can't remember.' He clearly strained to smile. His apparent uneasiness bothered me. Had he guessed that with asking for his family tree information, which at the time he seemed a little hesitant to offer up, that I may have uncovered something from his past that he may or may not

292

have known about? The answer to that, would have to wait until the evening...

CHAPTER THIRTY-SIX

Thursday 20th April 2023
19:37
At home, Knutsford

I heard the front door close. The lounge door opened and Chloe was stood in the doorway.

Her face lit up and she let out an involuntary yelp.

'Hello you,' she said all giddy girl like. 'I thought you were coming home tomorrow?'

'Changed my mind.'

'Well, a girl's allowed to change her mind isn't she.'

She gave me a meaningful and loving hug. I held her tightly; I thought about her life, and how it was about to change.

Smiling she released me from her embrace.

'I'll get a quick shower, slip into my PJs, and you can tell me all about it over a glass of wine.'

I smiled and nodded.

She stopped and turned.

'It's *great* to see you sis.'
I returned a heart-felt smile.
'You too Chloe.'

We gathered together in the conservatory. Glasses charged with a full-bodied red and nibbles placed on the table that my mum and me had put together…a sort of Mediterranean Mezze.
They all sat around me expectantly. I let out a sigh and smiled.
'Right.'

I went on to tell them that armed with the information that my dad had given me, and the research that Noah had done; I had managed to take our ancestry back in time. I left out all the other dramatic details. Although Chloe knew about the meeting of the stranger in Paris, Benoît, and his forewarning to me, and the real reason for retuning to Paris, I had to pick so carefully around every detail. Looking at her throughout the telling of the story, she understood I think that I was leaving out certain details for obvious reasons. She at that moment, had know idea just *how* much detail was being omitted. By the end of it I was shattered; not because it had been such a long day, but trying to avoid talking about everything, is not in my nature; it was mentally draining.

I looked around the table. Not for the first time over the past few days, a silence had fallen…

To make the family tree a little easier to understand, I had drawn out a basic tree. I would sit down and add all the children, dates and locations that I had learned, in a few days time when the dust has settled. I did though mention that George was in the SOE and Thomas MI5, but that due to the very nature of their clandestine activities, I hadn't found out any more detail than that. The questioning expression and look of doubt on Chloe's face would be answered later in the evening, when we were on our own…

England

Andrew Garner – Father

Thomas Garner - Grandfather

George Garner – Great Grandfather

Henry Garner – G G Grandfather

France

Louis Rochambeau
Wife – Yevette Garnier (Gar-nee-yay)
Children:
Yevette
Henry
Céleste

Thomas Rochambeau/de Merclesden

Richard de Merclesden

Robert de Merclesden, and his wife Alice

I looked at my dad. He was smiling. I couldn't be certain, but I felt that there was somewhat of a relief on his face that more had not been uncovered: that there were no skeletons in the closet. Little did he know of course. It was an awfully big closet; with an awful lot of skeletons.

My dad was clearly impressed.

'*Wow*! I had no idea about the French connection Alice. No idea at all. That's *extraordinary*. And that my father and grandfather had worked in the secret services...well, that's utterly overwhelming news to me. I can't believe that my father had not mentioned *any* of that to me. I can't possibly imagine why?'

I could!

He continued, 'And that Hugh de Rochambeau did the charitable act of adopting Thomas de Merclesden after his father Richard had died so bravely in battle,' (I had been a little moderate with the truth there, being an author has its benefits) 'it makes me so very proud of my ancestry. Thank you Alice. This means so much to me, more than I can tell you. I don't know why, but I had the feeling that things had not gone well with my ancestors. You have put that right, and I thank you for that.'

I mean; what do you do? There are times when you have to balance the truth with the pain it will cause,

298

and face the consequences; or remain silent, or bend it a little to have a kinder outcome. All in all, I think it worked out quite well.

The probing look on Chloe's face however, was going to need a little more thought and subtlety.

I had thought more carefully what I would say to her. I don't wish to lie to my sister: I *love* my sister and she me. The truth is however; she knows an awful lot more than my mum and dad and deserves to know the truth of it. I will of course, leave out what has transpired with the *rat* that walks the Earth, known as Noah.

CHAPTER THIRTY-SEVEN

Thursday 20th April 2023
22:38
Knutsford

Mum and dad had turned in for the night leaving Chloe and I sat together in the lounge.

Chloe poured out a small glass of wine for me and then for herself. She sat back and looked at me shrewdly and searchingly.
'Right you.'
I smiled and nodded
'OK.'

With the exception of Noah, I told her *everything* that had happened…

Throughout the retelling, she sat silently and without interruption, *absolutely* absorbed in what I was saying to her. She was lucky in a way; she was getting it in one hit. Not as it had with me; seeping and creeping up on me.

She sat on the sofa undeniably mesmerised and dumbstruck.

I looked at her and smiled.

'Another drink?'

'Erm…erm…yes. *Of course* I want another drink!'

I poured out a little more wine for her and sat back down on the sofa.

'That's a lot of information to process Alice. You must have been *terrified*. Why didn't you tell me?'

'What could you have done Chloe?'

'Well, I could have come out…or supported you in some way.'

'Truth is, it all happed so fast that I, we, didn't have time to think.'

She gave me a serious, yet thoughtful look.

'Are you in danger Alice?'

I shook my head.

'I don't have the letter. It didn't reach me. Pierre thinks that as I am not in possession of it, I am no longer at risk.'

'You can't be absolutely sure though?'

I raised my eyebrows.

'After what I've been through and what you've just listened to; can *any of us* be sure about anything?' Or anyone? I thought to myself.

'Hmm. Still, I don't know Alice?'

301

'Well, I can say tha…' my phone ringing interrupted me. I looked at the caller, and smiled.

'Hello Pascal.' I looked at Chloe. Her right eyebrow was raised and she had a stupid grin on her face as she mimed the name, Pascal, and formed her lips into a kiss.

I laughed.

Pascal's response…

'No sorry Pascal. I am with my sister Chloe. She just did something really childish.' Chloe narrowed her eyes and smirked once again.

response…

'No it's OK. I have just told her everything.'

response…

I looked at Chloe.

'No. How are you?'

response…

'Good. Yes I'm fine. I only stayed in Dartmouth for a night. I arrived home earlier this afternoon.'

response…

'It was tricky and I felt bad about it, but I told my mum and dad what I thought they needed to know.'

response…

I nodded my head.

'Yes you're right Pascal. It does seem to have been a pattern with this journey. People being a little creative with the truth.'

302

response…

A sudden chill ran down my spine.

'Say that again please Pascal,' I said, in a hushed voice.

response

'Are you absolutely sure Pascal?'

response…

'OK.'

response…

'I'll phone you tomorrow.'

response…

'Yes. Goodnight Pascal. Love you.' I looked at Chloe. Her eyes widened perceptibly. With the news I'd just been given, I couldn't focus momentarily. That's the excuse anyway for the little end of call sentiment.

'Love you?' echoed Chloe. Sporting a sassy smirk.

I held up the palms of my hands questioningly.

She wouldn't let it go.

'Love you?'

'OK. I get it. It just slipped out.'

'Yes. But…*lurve* you.'

'Shut up Chloe,' I said tongue-in-cheek.

She laughed and stood up.

'Coffee?'

I nodded.

'Coffee would be good.'

She stood and walked into the kitchen. It gave me a few moments in which to process what Pascal had just told me. He had received a phone call to confirm that his father had been knocked down and killed by a known drug dealer. Apparently, CCTV footage had shown him to be on his phone when he hit Benoît. As he drove away the police know that he contacted another drug dealer. They had met up and set the car alight. It was a tragic accident. It was manslaughter, but not the pre-arranged and calculated murder that Pierre, Pascal and I, had thought it to be. It now appeared that Noah had nothing to do with Pascal's father's death. I have to say that I was relieved. I didn't want him to be whom I thought him to be...a manipulative and scheming killer. He was though never the less, a liar and had misled me, and more importantly, Chloe.

'There we are.' Chloe placed the coffees on the table. 'Nice and strong.'

I looked at her.

'I love you Chloe.'

'*Bloody hell*! That trip to France has turned you into a bit of a hippy I think. You're lovin' *everyone*.'

We both laughed. I think because of the evenings revelations; rather more enthusiastically than we would have normally.

'So?'

I looked at her.

'So, what?'

'Pascal?'

'What about Pascal?'

'You know,' she said suggestively.

I smiled warmly. I do like him; I like him a lot. But I don't know yet?'

'Don't let the grass grow Alice. I mean, I nearly did with Noah. I'm so glad I said yes to meeting him again after the first date. I very nearly didn't.'

A sense of foreboding came over me. I managed a warm smile.

'Yes. Well. We'll see.'

She gave me an impish smile.

'I think *I* already know Alice.'

Changing tack…

'Dartmouth was fabulous. I can't think for the life of me why we don't use the house more than we do.'

'Funny that.'

'What is?'

'I didn't know that you were in Dartmouth; obviously,' she said, with raised eyebrows and a hint of sarcasm, 'but I thought about going down there next week with Noah. I've got a few days off. He's never been. I think he'd like it there.'

I nodded.

'Yes. I'm sure he would.'

She nodded.

'Yeah. That's a plan.'

'When is he back in the UK?'

'He's supposed to be flying back on Saturday. But, I spoke with him earlier. He said that his research had been concluded and that there was nothing to keep him there any longer than needs be. He's flying back tomorrow.'

"Concluded" I bet he's *desperate* to get back and find out what I have discovered. I was very much looking forward to having *that* conversation. It would however, have to be with him, alone, but somewhere public. I still don't trust him as far as I can spit! Benoît's death must have thrown a real spanner into the works. Then my sudden disappearance. I wonder if he knew where, and with whom, I went next?

'Actually you might be able to do me a favour?' she said.

'Sure. What is it?'

'You couldn't possibly pick him up from the airport could you?'

I had to think on my feet…and not for the first time! I was becoming quite the expert in the art of the impromptu.

'What time does his flight arrive?'

'Erm…' She picked up her phone from the table. '14:30.'

'Oh. Sorry Chloe. I can't. I've arranged to meet up with Daisy in Altrincham for a bit of retail.'

'Oh OK. No worries. He can get a taxi.'

I nodded.

The thought of being alone with him in my car filled me with an uneasiness and antagonism. If it was a novel that was unfurling, I might just be tempted to push him out of the door on the motorway and have done with it. Although, I'm not sure how I could write myself out of that one?

I had tried to remember her shift for the following week. She had told me last weekend and I was hoping I was on the nail.

'I've got a little time free next Monday morning. I was thinking of you and Noah having a catch-up coffee?'

'Oh I can't' Alice. I'm on shift. There's no reason why you and Noah can't meet up. I'm sure he'd *love* to hear what you've discovered.'

I wasn't so sure.

'It's not as though I would be missing anything having just heard it.'

I nodded.

'I'll speak to him tomorrow.'

'Ok Thanks Chloe. If you don't mind?'

She laughed.

'Why should I mind?'

I nodded and smiled.

'OK. Thanks.'

There was a short pause in the conversation before Chloe let out a deep sigh.

'What a *thing* though Alice.'

'Amen to that statement.'

'You did *really* well missing out quite a lot when you told mum and dad. I don't know how you worked that out?'

'Hey. I'm a writer…it's what we do.'

'Hmm. Even so.'

I laughed.

Chloe continued, 'Speaking of which, how's your new book coming along?'

It was my turn to let out a sigh.

'To be honest…I don't know. All that has happened has, well…I don't know.'

'Behind the masque, isn't it; the title?'

I nodded.

'Yeah.'

'It's a good title.'

I nodded in agreement.

'How are things with you Chloe?'

She looked a little uncertain.

'Do you mean with Noah and me?'

'*No,*' I said rather to expediently, which shocked her slightly, 'Sorry, I meant, at the hospital?'

'All good. I had a mid-term assessment on Tuesday.'

'Oh I didn't know. Sorry.'

'I didn't mention it. And you were away.'

'You *never* tell me.'

She laughed.

'I know. I don't like to put pressure on myself by the expectations of others.'

'We wouldn't do that Chloe.'

'I know you wouldn't. But, you know, it's my way of thinking.'

I shook my head and smiled.

'How did it go then?'

'Oh it went really well.'

I smiled.

'Why would it not?'

'Oh believe me, it could take just one small mistake and that could make all the difference.'

'Really.'

She nodded.

'Yes. Absolutely.'

'It is a lot of pressure isn't it Chloe.'

'It's medicine. You can't afford to make mistakes. They could have grave consequences. The tuition, instruction and guidance, *has* to be thorough and robust. All junior Doctors know that. It's what we sign up to.'

'I have nothing but respect Chloe.'

'And love apparently,' she said, impishly.

309

Once again we broke into spontaneous laughter. I had *really* enjoyed this conversation with my sister, albeit a little abnormal and revelatory in nature.

I let out an involuntary yawn.

'Well I don't know about you, but I'm done in.'

'I'm sorry Alice. It has been a long day for you, and a *hell* of a journey.'

I couldn't disagree with that.

'Still,' she smirked. 'Pascal,' she said seductively.

I picked up a cushion and playfully threw it at her.

We both laughed.

We tided everything away, and crawled up to our beds. As my head hit the pillow, my mind was now focused on what I would say to Noah. I didn't think on it too long however; I was out like a light…

CHAPTER THIRTY-EIGHT

Monday 24th April 2023
10:15
Courtyard Coffee House
Knutsford

I had arranged to meet Noah at 11:30 but arrived early to chill with a coffee and get my mind in order, and focussed on what I was going to say to him. I had one shot at this. It had to be right…

As I had arrived, the chef was lighting the logs of an outside roasting grill in preparation for the occasional lunchtime roast.

I was enjoying my coffee when a female voice from behind, punctuated my reverie.

'Hello.'

I turned and smiled thinking it was the waitress. It was a woman who I had never before set eyes on.

'May I sit down?'

I looked around me. Other than a middle-aged couple that were just leaving; there were no other customers...there was plenty of free tables and chairs.

She gave me an honest smile and asked me the same question.

'May I sit down Alice?'

My name being spoken by a total stranger; unnerved me and took me right back to the *Jardin des Plantes* and the first encounter I had with Benoît. I was however, intrigued and I was on home turf.

'Yes. But I am expecting a friend.' Well, I said friend, but he was not the friend I thought him to be the last time we sat together here.

The woman pulled out a chair and sat down. I looked at her. Whoever she was, she had bright and kind eyes. I waited for her to speak first.

'*Cognoscere hostem tuum.*'

I looked at her trying my hardest to not reveal to her through an easy-to-read facial expression, that at that moment, my heart was trying to smash its way out through my rib cage. I looked around me as the waitress came over to the table.

'Good morning,' she said to the woman, with a smile. 'Can I get you anything?'

She looked up and gave her an earnest smile.

'No thank you. I was just passing and saw my friend here. I thought I'd just say hello. Thank you all the same.'

'You're welcome. If you change your mind; I'll be just inside.' She turned and walked back into the coffee house.

'Just passing?' I said. 'We are in a courtyard. How does that work then?'

She smiled. And still I had no idea who she was? But she, quite clearly knew me.

'*Non sum inimicus tuus*. I really am not your enemy Alice.'

Here we go again, I thought rather too flippantly. 'Have we met?'

She gave me an unpretentious and genuine smile. She nodded.

'Yes. Albeit fleetingly.'

'I would have remembered meeting you?'

'We didn't meet as such. I walked by you.'

'That's no basis to turn up, sit down at my table and start quoting Latin.'

She smiled.

'Défenseur de la Foi?'

She nodded.

'What is it with you people. Destroying people's lives.'

'Quite the opposite Alice.'

'Sorry, that might have been a little harsh, but…you know.'

'I understand Alice.'

'So. You're not here for the coffee?'

'I last saw you when Benoît had just left you in *Jardin des Plantes*. You had been sat with him for a while discussing…' she hesitated, '…matters.'

'Matters?'

'Yes. He had just left you, when you said out loud, "the letter".'

I thought for a moment. Benoît had forgotten to give me the letter. Then I remembered a woman walking past as I'd said that, and she looked a little surprised.

'I remember you.'

She nodded.

'You have been following me ever since?'

She shook her head.

'No. But that was the first occasion we knew that Benoît was the bearer of the letter.'

'Who are you?'

'I think you just told me Alice.'

I shook my head.

'No. I mean who *really* are you?'

She tipped her head to one side thoughtfully and smiled.

'Défenseur de la Foi, is not all you have been led to believe. Pierre knows quite a lot; a little more than

Pascal. But Benoît knew so much more. I can tell you this. Our order goes back before the slaughter of Béziers. It is complicated and too much information to last the length of a coffee, but, simply put. Have you heard of the Knights Templar?'
'Yes I have.'
'It is well documented in modern day writing and of course in film, that there is a belief that whilst on crusade in Jerusalem, they discovered something of great significance. It was of such dramatic importance that it was presumed, that if revealed and used by the immoral, dishonest and evil; it could change the very fabric of society...our World...our humanity. There is truth in that modern day belief Alice. It comes from much older and ancient times.'
'Do you know what it is?'
She shook her head.
'It could be an artefact, a key, a code, a map, a manuscript, diary or a premonition: a forewarning of something that is going to happen. Whatever it was they found, the Templars passed on to the Cathars for safekeeping. The Church and state were about bring the power of the Templars, to a bloody and brutal end.'
I nodded.
'I know a little bit of that from my own ancestry...well, I do *now* at least.'

315

She continued, 'however, the Cathars and Jews themselves, became targets of ruthlessness, cruelty and genocide. Purely by chance, hearing your exclamation about the letter, we knew that Benoît held the key to the puzzle.'

'Loose ends?'

She looked a little perplexed.

'I'm sorry?'

I shook my head.

'Nothing. It was nothing. Different organisation. Please continue.'

'We had always promised protection for all those of our affiliation in our order. For centuries, it has been that way.' She stopped and hung her head. 'I wasn't there for Benoît. I couldn't save him from that.'

'It was an accident. Tragic yes; but an accident non-the-less. You couldn't have foreseen that.' Then a sudden realisation. 'You were *there*; on the bridge, when it happened. *You* took the letter.' She looked at me, and then reached down into her handbag. She placed the letter on the table. I looked down at it. It had my name on it. Yet again my heart was pounding. I shook my head.

'No. No no no. You keep it. Thanks all the same.'

'You are meant to have it. Benoît knew that.'

'*Meant* to have it? I mean…what does that even *mean*? Why me? Why not my father, or my grandfather; or *you*!'

'We don't choose who is the bearer Alice. It is not passed down through ancestry, knowledge or desire. It is given to the one who has been chosen.'

'Chosen? And who decides *that* exactly?'

She smiled.

'We don't know.'

'*Brilliant!* What an excellent answer. That gives me great comfort. Well, you can give it to someone else. I don't want it.'

'I, we, don't know why it has been passed to you? Maybe Benoît knew, maybe he didn't? We will never know that.'

Once again, I looked down at the letter on the table. She stood up.

'It is for you to decide Alice? Think upon it?'

'How do I know if it's for me to open or to be passed on again to some unsuspecting victim in the future?'

She gave me a heartfelt smile.

'Not victim Alice.'

'Well, it feels that way to me. Pushing a new life on someone against his or her will. Doesn't that make you a victim?'

'Victim is someone who is wounded, a casualty or prey. You are none of those Alice. This offer is something wonderful.'

'I'm sorry. I don't see it like that.'

'It is for you to decide Alice. All I ask is that you give it a little time and thought.'
'Goodbye Alice. I'm sure we will meet again.'
She just up and left me! I couldn't believe that's what she just did. She entered my life, left me with something out of The Da Vinci Code, and left! I was gobsmacked. After all that had happened; the letter was sat in front of me, with *my* name on it! I just stared at it...
'Hello Alice.'
I was shocked into life. I looked up. It was Noah. It was too late to move the letter out of sight. It would only look suspicious if I did that...so I left it on the table.
He looked at the letter and then to me. On the face of it he didn't seem to have a clue.
'Coffee?' I asked.
'Love one.'
The waitress came over to the table.
I looked at Noah.
'Erm, a flat white please.'
She looked to me.
'I'll have the same as before. Thank you?'
'Is there anything else I can get you?'
I answered for the both of us.
'No thank you.'
Noah seemed a little taken-aback. I on the other hand, suspected that his stay would be short.

318

'Thank you.' She turned and walked back inside.

'She's very courteous and polite.'

I nodded.

'Yes she is. Every time I come here she has a wonderful sincere smile and always takes time out to make you feel comfortable.'

There was an awkward silence momentarily…

'It's a pity Chloe was working today,' he said.

'Yes. Being a doctor is a calling I guess. It doesn't really run to a clock as such, as it does with most jobs.'

He sat smiling and nodding his head like one of those nodding dogs in the back window of a car of the 1970s and 80s. Sitting with him, was making me feel a little nauseous to be honest. I wanted to get this over with as soon as I could. I wasn't sat here to exchange pleasantries with him.

'So Alice.'

'So Noah?'

'What did you discover in France? Have you been able to add anymore to your family history?'

I could feel my blood boiling.

I forced a smile.

'Oh yes. Quite a *lot* actually.'

His eyes widened.

'Really?'

I nodded enthusiastically.

'Yes.'

The waitress walked over to us carrying a small tray with the coffees on board. She placed the coffees on the table put the tray under her arm, smiled and headed back inside.

'Well Alice?'

'Well what Noah?'

'Come on Alice. Don't keep me in suspense.'

Now was the time!

'Well, Noah Wexler, or should that be…Dreschsler?'

I've never seen blood drain from a person's face so quickly. I thought he might have a thrombosis there and then. I looked at him indifferently and continued, 'Noah Wexler, descendant of Franz and Charles or Karl, if you prefer, Dreschsler. Nice ancestry you have inherited Noah.'

He sat back in his chair; his first initial shock becoming an expression of resignation. He smiled.

I leaned in towards him and lowered my voice. 'Don't you smile at me you bastard!'

His eyes widened. He tried to lean further back into his chair to escape me. I sat back again and he seemed a little more relaxed. I gave him a few moments to digest what had just happened…

After all he had said to me about my family, he now apparently seemed lost for words. He looked at me. 'Well done Alice. You worked it out.'

'With a little help from my, *true* friends. Yes.'

He looked down at the letter on the table; then to me.

'That's it...isn't it?'

I nodded and slid it under my hand and then towards me.

'Do you know what that is Alice?'

'Does anyone?'

'It is the answer to everything.'

I looked at him. I was full of rage but did not want him to see that he had the upper hand. Calmly, I continued, 'whatever this is Noah, it is responsible for so many deaths, family disintegration, lies, deceit, treachery, pain...' I thought about Thomas's incarceration in Wiesbaden...' immeasurable and indescribable pain, and dehumanisation that has come down through the centuries. And has for countless generations, destroyed people in its wake. *No!* I'm wrong. It is not the letter or what it contains or represents: it's the selfish, cold-hearted, ruthless, brutal and merciless people that have coveted, whatever it contains; not unlike yourself; and for *what*? Power, control, dominance, wealth; all of the above? A friend once said to me, and it is so appropriate for where we find ourselves now...*Cui bono*. Who benefits?'

He just stared at me. After all his scheming and manipulating the truth...he could say nothing. With the letter in my hand, I looked at the building. I stood up, and looked at him. A look of absolute disbelief and horror set across his face.

'*Don't Alice. Don't* do it!'

'It ends here Noah. Now,' I said, calmly.

'*No* Alice! *Please*. You don't know what you are *doing*!'

'I'm doing something that is long overdue.'

The waitress looked out of the window, but didn't come out.

I think he was in *so* much shock and disbelief of what I was about to do, that he was unable to move any of his limbs and prevent me. I walked over to the grill and put the letter on top of heated logs. It ignited and instantaneously erupted into flame. I turned and looked at Noah. His head was lowered, and his hands cupped around his face. The waitress came out. She looked concerned.

'Is everything OK?'

'Yes. I think we are leaving now. Could I settle the bill please.'

'Erm…yes of course.'

I followed her inside and took out my debit card to pay. I placed my card on the card reader and looked over to the table…Noah had gone.

'Thank you,' she said.

I looked at the chard embers of the letter still spiralling in the air.

'Good fire,' I said with a smile. 'Good bye.'

'Good bye,' she echoed, 'and thank you.'
I turned and smiled contentedly.

CHAPTER THIRTY-NINE

Wednesday 26th April 2023
08:15
Tatton Park
Knutsford

Sitting quietly here by the Mere in Tatton Park; is healing me. Since Monday, after the letter and grill occasion, I had begun to unpack my psychological and spiritual baggage. For the first time since dropping my book off at Shakespeare and Company, Paris, I had found peace and normality. I had even thought about my book, Behind the Masque.

The irony is of course, that it began its life set in 18th Century Venice and I wanted to include within the story:

Intrigue
Betrayal
Vengeance
An affair
Theft of idea
Hidden child's identity
Family deceptions
Stolen inheritance
Merchants
Incarceration
And a long kept secret.

Most of the above storylines, plots and subplots for the novel, have already played out in my own family history. I'm not really feeling it any more to be honest.

The masque of the title, were masks worn at carnivals and Masque balls by different social classes allowing them to mingle without fear of identification, justice or reprisals. Not unlike the thread that has run through this story: behind the Masque of respectability, decency and loyalty, lay, betrayal, treachery and vengeance. However, it also showed me a different side to human nature; that of kindness, caring, compassion and the willingness to risk all, to help another human being. There is no need for me to write the book; it has already been written.

Noah and Chloe saw each other the day after I had been at the Courtyard Coffee House with him. Unsurprisingly, he then disappeared. Chloe has yet to tell me why she is so upset…and I respect her enough to not ask her. I know of course; but she will tell me when she's ready.

I know I did the right thing with the letter; many would disagree I'm sure. But there it is. I leave the judgment for you to decide.

As for Pascal and I…we shall see what the future brings. I have a good feeling about our future lives.

For most of us, there is a hidden, historical, subterranean World running beneath our lives. It is probably just as well that we are unaware of it; as it allows us a familiarity and routine, in which to live out our lives, in the here, and now.

Protinus vive

Printed in Great Britain
by Amazon